G. S. (George Slythe) Street

The Wise and the Wayward

G. S. (George Slythe) Street

The Wise and the Wayward

ISBN/EAN: 9783337002077

Printed in Europe, USA, Canada, Australia, Japan

Cover: Foto ©Andreas Hilbeck / pixelio.de

More available books at **www.hansebooks.com**

THE WISE

AND

THE WAYWARD

THE WISE

AND

THE WAYWARD

BY

G. S. STREET

JOHN LANE: THE BODLEY HEAD
LONDON AND NEW YORK
1896

SECOND EDITION.

University Press:
JOHN WILSON AND SON, CAMBRIDGE, U.S.A.

CONTENTS

The Wise and the Wayward

CHAPTER I

A CONVERSATION

OLD Mrs. Ashton of Rowe and Mr. Wilmot, her oldest friend, sat and talked after dinner. They sat out of the range of the lamps, but the light of the big fireplace of the big drawing-room of Rowe House shone on Mrs. Ashton's little lace cap and neat white hair and delicate small face as she leaned thoughtfully over the blaze and held her hands to its warmth. She was always cold, and the little shiver visible whenever she moved a yard from a fire seemed consistent with the glance of indefinable inquietude which met an intimation of outside things — outside the quiet house where she read old letters and mused over the fire and thought on future happiness or

devised present comfort for George Ashton, her
son.   She had been out in the cold in her time,
and was come to think the warmth of the fire
the thing most desirable for herself and for those
who were dear to her, and she shivered when
they vaunted the winter weather.   A gentle and
appealing old lady, fragile, dignified, and loved.

It was a pity, artistic effect considered, that
Francis Wilmot was not her husband.   He was
the complement, in a favourable sense, of her
sweet old age.   He was tall, straight, and ruddy,
and a natural grace alone saved the youthfulness
of his sixty-eight years from aggressiveness.
His hair, as white as his old friend's, was brushed
back in a broad sweep from his forehead, and
was an appropriate contrast with his thick eyebrows, still black, and his black keen eyes.   He
was clean-shaven.   He stood with his back to
the fire and tapped the hearth-rug with a small,
shining pump.   A virile, fine old man, who
laughed at his own strong prejudices and never
questioned them.   As he looked down with a
quiet, protective affection on the small old lady,
he should have been her husband.   But her
husband had been a subtle-minded fault-finder, a
drunkard, and a wayward amorist, and had died

at fifty. It was something that Francis Wilmot
was her oldest friend.

They were talking of George Ashton's engagement to marry, announced to Mrs. Ashton on his
arrival that afternoon.

"Francis," the old lady said, "tell me; you
don't like it?"

"I? I think it's time he married. Thirty,
is n't he? And a man with a place like this
ought to marry."

"Your place is larger."

Mr. Wilmot looked kindly upon her and spoke
gaily: —

"And I have n't even had the sense of duty
to marry! A useless old idler!" — The lady
smiled softly at him and looked back at the fire.
— "But I'm a bad example; neglected every
other duty too."

"Except being the best landlord in your
county and the best friend in the world."

"Oh, nonsense; I'm what the Socialists call
an encumbrance to the community; never done
a stroke of work — "

"Francis, I want to talk about my boy."

"With all my heart. You know what I think
of him. With his father's brains and your dis-

position — I beg your pardon very humbly,
Dorothy — with your brains — "

"Francis, why do you evade me? You can
say anything to me. I don't know these people;
I can't help feeling nervous. You must tell me
what you know."

"That is almost nothing. I used to know
Canover slightly; I have seen his daughters;
George has chosen a wonderfully pretty girl.
You must n't think he has done anything foolish.
It's the idea of his caring for anybody more than
you that makes you anxious — "

"I think not. I am not a strong woman,
perhaps, but I am not stupid or blind. George
has had fancies before — he never tells me, but
I know. I don't deceive myself about his
character. He's the best son in the world, and
an honourable man. But about women he is
easily governed by the feelings that pass. The
women who have attracted him have sometimes
— I speak vaguely, you understand — sometimes not been those whom his judgment and
his delicacy would choose. It may be so now.
I must be unhappy till I know. It's not parting
with him — we must part in a way — I knew
that must come. I have only prayed that his

wife will let me love her and not put barriers between my son and me. I am unhappy till I know he has chosen well. Tell me what you know, dear friend."

"My dear, I should never forgive myself if I said anything to make mischief in the least degree. I will be absolutely frank with you. You know I think a great deal of George, and I have known him very well all his life. Naturally, then, I am not easily satisfied that his wife is good enough for him. I simply don't happen to know that Miss Canover is: that is really all."

Mrs. Ashton smiled sadly. "Diplomatist! What of Major Canover?"

"Since he's left the army he's been doing something in the City. No, Dorothy, you're a woman in a million. It's best to tell you all I know; you're safe to hear it somewhere. Canover is *not* a good fellow, though he's pleasant enough. He's been mixed up with things pretty near the wind, and there was one case which got into the law courts — the other people concerned were a money-lender and a very young man. And he has not done well by his daughters. Their mother died when they were children, and since they've been out Canover has exploited them in a way, hawked them about, made them seem a sort of quasi-professional beauties. I'm talking like a malicious old gossip, but these are facts everybody will tell you. They don't tell against the girl in the least. I know nothing whatever against her. Perhaps some busybody will tell you she has had a few harm- less flirtations: there's nothing more. Very likely George is the first man she has really cared for. That and your influence — "

The hater of scandal was a trifle out of breath. He looked troubled ; he had really spoken as he thought right, but wondered if he had said too much. Mrs. Ashton passed her hand across her eyes.

"Poor girl!" she said. "But my boy — he is so sensitive."

"Here he comes. We were talking about you, George."

George Ashton bent over his mother and kissed her as he passed to the fire. He was a little above the average in height, slight, thin- featured, with large greyish-blue eyes and light brown hair, and a broad forehead. His look was frank, but not alert; one was not sure of an im- pression : it might be of brains and taste, it might

hardly be of vigour or determination. The effect
was faintly ironical; the little laugh with which
he answered Mr. Wilmot was not merry; there
were slight lines at the corners of his mouth.

"Of course you were. And about my marriage and happiness ever after. Mr. Wilmot has
been telling you lots of charming things about
Nell, I'm sure, mother."

"I only know her looks, my boy."

"No?" There was the faintest possible tinge
of defiance in his voice. "But you know the Major? He said he knew you. H'm! Poor Francis,
you need n't be embarrassed. I don't swagger
about the Major, but I suppose he'll do the
heavy father as well as another. I don't marry
the family. But you will like Nell, mother."

Mrs. Ashton went to her son and looked up
into his eyes.

"Yes, mother dear. I know the atmosphere
she's lived in is antipathetic to you, but she's
not part of it. She's fond of gaiety and that sort
of thing, of course, but it's never spoiled her.
She has a straight, simple nature. Yes, mother,
she's a noble girl; she is indeed."

"Yes, dear," said Mrs. Ashton, while Francis
Wilmot looked gravely at his shining pumps.

CHAPTER II

ANOTHER CONVERSATION

THE Ashtons of Rowe were not a distinguished family. They had lived at Rowe some three hundred years — a tolerably long while for England — and had never fallen from their importance in their district of Hampshire. But no Ashton of Rowe survived in the memory of a grateful country as general, admiral, or statesman, although a few were of some account in their day. They had had their definite place in the English society of their times, and you meet them now and again in memoirs and letters. None of them, however, had shone brightly in social life, and for some generations they had lived almost entirely at Rowe, entertaining their neighbours, but not filling their house with guests.

Oddly, for two generations they had not been mighty sportsmen. George Ashton's father

and grandfather, though both strong men, and
active by fits and starts, had lived much in their
library, a type of well-bred and fastidious students
of literature, who would have been welcome at
Strawberry Hill.   It must have been love of
Rowe that made them its constant occupiers,
and Rowe was meet to be loved.   In all Hampshire there was no more perfect expression of a
gracious English life — a life dignified and somewhat retired, ordered and above ambition, artificial (doubtless) and soon to pass away.   For
mere wealth, the reward of struggle, and mere
friendliness of manner, which may remain, pro-
duce no such atmosphere as that of Rowe.

The house was Jacobean, formal and stately
in its approach, but at the back, where were
broad terraces and an abundance of flowers,
inviting and sympathetic.   The gardens merged
soon in the glades and avenues of the park.   A
large hall, the large drawing-room opposite,
two broad staircases at each end — imagine
some favourite country house, and the atmosphere which many generations of right
keeping may make for right imaginations.
Outside the park was the dower-house, an older
building covered with creepers, empty, since it

was an Ashton tradition not to let it, and George Ashton and his mother were people for whom such traditions have a value.

Since leaving Oxford, George Ashton had spent most of his time at Rowe with his mother, and the rest of it in his rooms in London. In London he was much as are most young men who like amusement and can afford to buy it. He belonged to a good club, dined out, danced occasionally in the season, and occasionally dived into what passes for Bohemia. Balliol had respected him, and, like his father and grandfather, he was fond of books and contemporary letters in a quiet fashion — worth mentioning in regard to a taste which is now-a-days somewhat curiously noisy — and at Rowe was absorbed in them. That he had escaped certain other of his father's tastes altogether, I cannot affirm. He was fond of wine, and amorous as well, but in both particulars he had improved on the paternal example, being neither scandalous nor a drunkard. Nor do I affirm that he was a useful member of society : I fear that my narrative has mostly to do with useless people. He had no profession, and did not really believe in the great work which, when written, should justify his existence. Yet he had a few stray virtues. Amusement had not spoiled his intellect, nor his intellect his manners. His devotion to his mother had involved no sacrifice of himself, but he loved her sincerely, and intimacy with her had opened and cherished a natural delicacy and good will to the world, which his life had sometimes jarred upon, but had left unspoiled.

Perhaps, however, it is more satisfactory to turn to his first cousin, John, his senior by a few years and, failing a son, his heir. For Jack Ashton was that thing most acceptable to men, and, let us hope, to heaven, a person in complete harmony with his environment, absolutely and unremittedly content. His wife had the same pre-eminence, and so, apart from the inevitable woes of babyhood, had their year-old boy. Husband and wife were fond of each other and of the baby, and the baby was as fond of them as could be expected. It is therefore my privilege to introduce you to a happy home.

Jack Ashton's father had married a woman of substantial fortune, and Jack Ashton followed his wise example. Having enjoyed himself thoroughly but wisely, he thought it well, at thirty-one, to double his income and make himself a permanent home by marrying the daughter (aged twenty-five) of a successful promoter of companies. She in her way had enjoyed life as thoroughly and wisely, and also was aware of the common sense in the contract. He was strong and handsome, and attracted her; she was handsome and healthy, and attracted him. Their tastes and their aims in life were very like. Solid pleasures appealed to them both, and especially the pleasure of pleasant eating, a taste of which the value for harmony cannot be exaggerated. They both were fond of riding and the open air. Both were easily amused; no farce ever devised could have kept them from laughing. Both wished above all things to get all the pleasure their incomes could possibly procure; both were content with the fashion of the moment; both disliked and avoided eccentricity. The blood of commercial success and practical wisdom was strong in both. Jack spent an occasional hour on the direction of one of his father-in-law's companies, and fenced for an hour a day. Mildred spent an equal time on the affairs of their house and on her dresses. For the rest of the day they were a good deal in one another's company, eating,

seeing their friends, going to the play. Away
from London, they lived chiefly in other people's
houses, where an efficient sportsman and a jolly
and handsome woman were welcome. Occasionally they pecked at Paris or Monte Carlo.
I do not say theirs was a life of philanthropy
or in the vanguard of progress. They were
not remarkable for generosity or for loyalty to
friends in adversity. Their culture was certainly not of an advanced type. But they were
fond of and faithful to one another, and if we live
in a state of society in which the home is the
unit and the most important consideration, then
Jack Ashton and Mildred his wife were almost
perfect beings. If we do not so live, there may
be something to be said against them : that they
were selfish or so, that they were narrow. But
what does that matter? In due time the baby
arrived, and put a crown on this glory of domestic virtue.

You are privileged to contemplate it at about
half-past two in the afternoon, at its home in
Eaton Place. Jack Ashton and his wife had
finished lunch, a substantial and deliberately
considered lunch, and were looking with slightly
torpid affection on one another. Jack Ashton

was dark, sleek, and handsome in (possibly) a somewhat bovine manner. He looked athletic and in good condition, perhaps half a stone or so above his weight. His wife was a very plump but straight and well-made young woman, dark also, with clear, regular, and intelligent features, not quite undistinguished in general effect, well but imposingly dressed, a little lavishly ringed. A letter came for her, and she opened it and read.

"Oh, dear! Oh, Jack! George Ashton's going to marry!"

The two round faces were grave, and Jack stopped eating grapes in salute to the bad news.

"There goes my chance!" he said; "but of course it was always likely. Damn, though."

"Oh, I don't know. He used to shut himself up so at Rowe. Of course I never wished him any harm — still, you were the next — It *is* cruel — Oh, Jack, guess whom he's going to marry!" Her melancholy gave way to excitement. "It's *too* extraordinary."

"Who? He used to go about with Lady Tremayne. She's married though. Who is it?"

"You'll never guess. Nelly Canover!"

"*No!* By Jove, though, what! Nelly Canover! She'll make Rowe sit up, though, won't she?"

"I cut her only a month ago," said Mildred, reflectively, "when Lucy Skeffington would n't speak to her. I thought it best on the whole, and now Mrs. Ashton writes calmly to say her son's going to marry her. It's a jar for her — George's mother — is n't it?" She laughed mirthfully, and comfortably added, "I always hated her."

"Poor old lady, she has n't been bad to you, Milly."

"Oh, she presented me when we married, and gave me those stones. But she always seems to snub me. I can stand alone now. I wonder about those jewels of hers, though. They 're not heirlooms, are they?"

"No! why?"

"Why, don't you see, she 's sure to quarrel with Nelly Canover, and why should n't she leave them to me? That would be something, if I can't be Mrs. Ashton of Rowe. Her money too — One can't tell."

Jack Ashton was lost in the practical young woman's ready acceptance of the situation. The taste of it may have escaped him, or he may have recognised the beautiful confidence in himself which made it possible.

"But fancy George Ashton," she continued; "what could have made him do it?"

"Oh, she's pretty enough when all's said and done."

"But a man who lives alone on his place nine months in the year —"

"George isn't a saint, all the same. Besides, any man might fall in love with her."

"How did he know her?"

"I don't know; I remember now Skeffington told me he often met him there."

"Do you think he knows all about her?"

"George?" asked the sagacious Jack, "Oh, he must. After all, it's only that she's been mixed up with a few men who haven't the best reputation in the world. There's nothing very definite against her."

Mrs. Jack compressed her lips. "H'm!" she said. "Well, I'll go and call on the Canovers this afternoon."

"Will she like it after your cutting her?"

"Oh, that was a mistake. She can't do without me, under the circumstances, and it's no use our being at feud with Rowe."

"By Jove," her husband remarked, after a pause, " I should n't be surprised if she bolted at the church-door or something. She's wild enough."

Mildred smiled but shook her head. " She can't be such a fool. And with a man like George it's no use trying — anybody's trying — to break it off." She sighed as a resigned sufferer.

" But they're sure to quarrel afterwards. Perhaps after all — " here Jack remembered his magnanimity and delicacy — " but hang it, it's not our business. We must try to make things comfortable, you know."

" Ye—es," said his wife. She leaned her cheek on her hand and toyed with the grapes on her plate, meditating. Then brightly she rose and went across to her husband.

" Well, old boy, we must cheer ourselves up. We'll dine out to-night. Most of the dinner will do for lunch to-morrow. We'll dine somewhere together and go to a play." She patted her husband's cheek; he took the cigar from his mouth, and they kissed one another. Let us leave them in this position of domestic tenderness.

2

CHAPTER III

A WOMAN'S REFLECTIONS

1000 LOWNDES STREET, S. W.
Tuesday.

DEAR GEORGE, — I congratulate you on attaining
the wish of your heart and wish you every happiness
with all mine. When shall I meet Miss Canover?
Soon, I hope. I used to know her mother some centuries ago, and feel a very old, old woman. I go down
to Beckley to hunt for a fortnight to-morrow, but hope
when I return you will, when you are in town, bring
Miss Canover to see your ancient friend. My best
remembrances, please, to Mrs. Ashton, and Believe
me,   Ever sincerely yours,

CLARA TREMAYNE.

IT was a commonplace letter enough, but
when Lady Tremayne had finished it, she paused
to consider its fitness. She read it through
twice, and then threw it down. She looked
rather vacantly before her, then quickly folded
and addressed it. As she rose from the small

bureau in a corner of her long, twisted drawing-room — it took advantage of the angle in a corner-house — and walked towards the fire, she seemed — as you would guess from her allusion to her old age — very young for her thirty-five years. She was tall, slender, and her face, a little long in feature, was of a beauty that, for want of the right word, we call intellectual and spiritual. Though she walked erect and firmly, there was about her some suggestion of ethereal mystery. Whether, if you saw her hunting, and not, as now, in a sweeping tea-gown, the suggestion would be gone or would be intensified, I cannot tell. But I think such women as Lady Tremayne (whom I cannot hope to describe) carry always in their air, even in their intimate speech, a reserve which the perceptive know to be inevitable, and the coarse-grained either do not see or cannot tolerate. One assumes breeding, of course: there is another reserve, which is an infallible criterion of something to be avoided. Lady Tremayne was a sportswoman, a woman of brains, a woman of the world. When Jack Ashton, a casual acquaintance, met her, it never crossed his mind that she was less open to him than he to her; to Mildred Ashton she was detestable.

She sat in a low chair before the fire, and mused on her life. It was not the life of a heroine or a martyr. She had not married Sir Maurice Tremayne, her senior by nearly twenty years, to save her father from ruin or to educate her younger brothers. She married him, when she was twenty-seven, because she liked him, because she was tired of her mode of life, because she hated poverty, because she knew her world and saw in the future life no marvellous potentialities for which to forego this apparent certainty. In a way she was fortunate. Sir Maurice Tremayne was a soldier, interested in his profession and in politics. His wife gave him all, with one exception, which he had wished for and expected; to perform his part of the arrangement was no task to a courteous and even-tempered gentle-man. Her love of hunting, which he under-stood, he gratified; her love of books, which he did not understand, he did not obstruct. But there assiduity ended. She had borne him no child, and he felt no overpowering admiration for her mind or body. It was better so perhaps; a grey life is better than a yellow life of jealous trials, or a black life of unacceptable and constant love-making; but grey Lady Tremayne's life indubitably was. She had the keen but fleeting delight of hunting, she had the equable delight of a literary taste which cared nothing for fevered crazes. She was not a profoundly affectionate woman; but she had power to exercise and power to appreciate a delicate sympathy, and somehow there had come in her way little opportunity for either.

Into this grey life had come George Ashton. She had known him since her marriage, for Mrs. Ashton was an old friend of her husband, but it was only in the last two or three years that she had known him well. There are minds in these days to whom the mention of a man and a woman proves that a luckless story-teller implies some gross connection. They are minds which, as a poet has said, it is impossible to cleanse or to enlighten — one can but say they lie. There was no word or deed of George Ashton and Lady Tremayne concerning one another which could have pained Sir Maurice, her lord. They were fast friends. Their attitudes to their fellows were sympathetically diverse, the woman's aloof, sorrowful, a little bitter, the man's kindly, a little contemptuous, and aloof. Neither had sown in tears, neither had reaped in joy. Each felt, not very vaguely, what was lacking in the other's content, and each ministered somewhat to the want, the one knowing surely, but not deeply regretting, that no ministry could be complete, the other knowing, sorrowfully perhaps, that some other woman, not she, might minister wholly. Their talk was impersonal, a little personally so sometimes. They went about together, to the opera, to theatres sometimes, to see pictures. She, a matron and his senior, came to call him by his Christian name. They sat in the park together; they sat together in Lady Tremayne's drawing-room. When they met in society, they talked with one another almost invariably, and of course some people talked about them — in the colourless modern manner which may mean nothing, or may mean that nothing matters.

I am sure that George Ashton would have had no success had he tried to be more than a friend to Lady Tremayne. I am sure that she never suggested to herself a wish that he should try. I am not sure that, had he tried,

there would not have been some pleasure in
defeating him. He did not try. There are
men of facile passions with whom, given mere
possibility, intimacy and desire are always
joined. They are not of necessity coarse-
minded, for intimacy may precede; they are
men of facile passions. There are other men
with whom intimacy and desire are most often
separate — they are not the true antithesis of
the others, merely another kind of man —
whom, to speak roughly, sense and spirit (or
even, sometimes, the subtle and rare effects
of sense) attract in different places. George
Ashton was one of these: you may find a cause
possibly, but with dubious science, in the sensi-
tiveness and delicacy of his mother and his
father's exaggerated instinct. He had had
more than one commonplace amour, and more
than one subtle and searching and (as the
world will have it) innocent intimacy with a
woman. Clara Tremayne was the last of these.
The friendship satisfied George Ashton. I am
not sure that the friendship brought with it
perfect peace and contentment to the mind of
Clara Tremayne.

At last there happened a thing which had not

happened before, George Ashton thought. He
was in love with and desired to marry a girl
whom his best perceptions and intuitions allowed him to approve. This time, he told himself (I regret to say he had a habit, very shock-
ing to some people, of thinking about his
emotions), these intuitions and perceptions were
not in abeyance. It was true that Nelly Canover had lived a life he thought stupid and
rather vulgar, and that there were moments
when this fact was apparent in her conversation.
But below all that lay a spirit which was frank
and loyal, which he could unreservedly admire.
So much he told himself, and he added that the
delights and graces of her manner meant more
— so much more! — than a beauty which of
course was adorable. Yes! she was perfect;
it was hopeless to analyse her. Hers was a
union — to recur to my own brief summary —
of spirit and sense. He said as much in a more
concrete way in his letter of announcement to
Lady Tremayne, who of course was delighted
by such a consummation. She knew all that
the world in general knew of Nelly Canover,
whom Mildred Ashton had cut, and she wrote
the letter which began this chapter. She had a
right to say she was George Ashton's friend.

Clara Tremayne sat before the fire and mused on her life. The old life in Northamptonshire in her father's house, the hospitality, the sport, and the kindness, came back to her, and then the sorrow when the place had to be let, and the bitterness (to her mother as well) when her father, who loved his land more than his vanity, insisted on taking a small house near and being his own agent. How they had schemed to avoid going to their old home! They were unfortunate socially in their tenants, who were neither such as their own poverty could not have affected externally, nor honest tradesfolk who would have respected their birth and been glad of their countenance, but pseudo-"smart" cockneys who had made a showy marriage for the son of the house, and felt sure of the County without them. Clara Bruce-Chatterton retired into the world of books. Then one day Sir Maurice Tremayne, the famous and the rich, came home from India, to stay with his old friend in the small house, and the girls of the big house spread their nets before his eyes. I am not sure that the rebuke to those young persons was not one of the many reasons why Clara Bruce-Chatterton married him. Then came the

routine of the last eight years — courtesy, deco-
rum, quietude, the grand manner.   Ah! — All
her life, she mused, she had had the protection and guiding that she needed less than most
women, and had missed something intangible.

Back came her thoughts definitely to George
Ashton.   That boy — since his engagement,
he was steadily more youthful in her mind
— that boy had been a pleasant companion;
he was intellectual, sympathetic, tactful.   He
had often been unhappy; she had tried to be
a helpful friend to him.   He was very clever,
very straightforward, affectionate, and thoughtful for other people.   What a shame if he were
throwing his life away.   Nelly Canover perhaps
was only innocently fast: she was lovely, no
doubt; other men had made marriages less
hopeful even than this and had not been altogether spoiled by them.   Since these were her
placid and philosophical reflections, it is strange
that at this point in them Clara Tremayne
burst into tears.

CHAPTER IV

A LONDON INTERIOR

MAJOR CANOVER began the conversation by ramarking that the soup was vile. He sat at dinner with his two daughters at his house in Victoria Road, Kensington. A bald head and a heavy grey moustache suggested a stage major. His old age was not venerable, but red-faced, irascible, sparkish — a major possibly of farce. The beautiful Nelly was slight and admirably graceful. Her hair was red-brown, and her eyes were blue and large and dreamy; her face was perfectly oval; her nose was straight and rather short; her ears were minute; her mouth small, inclined to fulness. A rapt and beautiful angel she might be, or a very pretty, pouting girl. Kate, her elder sister, was a light-haired variety of Nelly, taller, less pretty, thinner.

"I shall take to dining at the club again," said Major Canover.

"Do," said his elder daughter; "dinner here costs about seven and six altogether; you can dine at the club for seven and four pence; Nelly and I can have a penny bun each."

This gloomy pleasantry was received with an inarticulate expression of suffering impatience by the Major, but Nelly laughed. "Poor old man," she said, "was his soup bad then, a dear!"

"Oh, it's all very well for you," said Kate; "you'll be out of it all in a month. We've got to stay on here."

"Yes," the Major added, slowly and half dubiously as he looked at Nelly; "we've got to stay on here."

"Oh, you'll come and stay with me," she responded colourlessly.

"Where's Ashton?" The Major's interest was not entirely hopeful.

"At Rowe; he's coming up to-morrow."

"I wonder what Mrs. Ashton's like," Kate said, thoughtfully.

"I'm sure she's a dear, and I'm going to love her tremendously."

"Will she go to the dower-house, I wonder? There is a dower-house, is n't there?"

" Really, Kate, how can I say?   I hope she 'll like to live with me."

" Oh, well, you know —" Kate laughed very slightly.

" What do you mean? " Her sister was eager. " If you mean I shall do anything against her, you 're wrong. My gratitude to George alone — "

" Gratitude ? "

" Yes, gratitude.   I 'm honest in this, Kate."

" Oh, you know best," Kate said, sourly.

Major Canover finished his soup, and pulled himself together.   He became genial and indulgent, as always when Kate was cross with Nelly. He liked the favourable contrast.

" George Ashton 's a good fellow," he said generously. " I think you 'll be happy, my dear. I 've done my best for you. Silver and gold have I none, but such as I have — God bless you, my child."   He beamed on her in silence, while the parlour-maid put the fish on the table.   But circumstances waged against him. " Whiting! if there is a fish on God's earth — no, thank you."   He rose and stood in front of the fire, lowering until the servant had left the room.

"Whiting! I slave in the city all day —"

"Oh, dear, dear; it's impossible to please you; I wish you'd order the dinner yourself," said Kate.

"Oh, hang the fish!" said Nelly.

"It's like eating the table-cloth — damn thing. What else is there? Boiled mutton, I've no doubt. What? upon my soul —"

"Oh, do talk about something else. Charlie Skeffington's coming this evening," Nelly interrupted.

"Is he? That reminds me." Major Canover was heavier at once. "What's this Kate tells me about Lady Skeffington's cutting you? What the devil does she mean?"

Nelly blushed and looked angrily at Kate. "Oh, nothing, father. It's only some silly fancy. I don't care. Charlie Skeffington apologised for her."

"In her name?" asked Kate, with a careless air.

"Oh, of course you want to make things as unpleasant as possible. It's really nothing father. Don't bother about it."

"My dear child, if your name got mixed up with Skeffington just as you're going to be mar-

ried, by Jove, it's — it's most unfortunate. Why
was he always coming here? You ought to have
looked after things better, Kate."

"I?" asked Kate indignantly, "I? *You*
brought Lord Skeffington here and told us particularly to be nice to him. You'd better speak
to him yourself."

For a moment Major Canover looked as if it
were his turn to blush. He cleared his throat,
and seemed relieved when the entrance of the
parlour-maid put an end to the discussion. The
boiled mutton escaped further animadversion,
and his voice was cheerful as he said: "I've
asked a man called Morrison to look in this
evening."

"Who and what is Morrison?"

"Oh, fellow I met in the city. Vulgar fellow,
rather. Rich fellow. Useful fellow — at least I
hope. Skeffington wants to meet him, by the
way. He's not so bad when you know him.
Rather heavy in hand, but a good-hearted fellow
— at least I think he is. He liked to be asked
here in an informal way, and that."

Kate sent a brief and half-contemptuous glance
towards her father. Nelly half frowned, and then
gave a little sigh of relief. She was to be married in a month.

They had not been long in the drawing-room after dinner when Lord Skeffington arrived. His native country, which paid him no rents, had favoured him with blue eyes and black hair; otherwise he looked a commonplace little man, with a little black moustache, with a bright expression, and with a sweet smile, which was frank as he shook hands with Nelly, faded a little for Kate, and took a faint line of irony as he greeted Major Canover. He was followed shortly afterwards by Mr. Morrison, a massive, sallow man, of a measured and somewhat greasy politeness, and a painful appearance of being in "full dress," who began without loss of time to impress his position upon his audience. Soon Nelly Canover and Lord Skeffington wandered into the little conservatory which led out of the room, and Skeffington sighed with hearty relief as he sat himself down by her side.

"What a beast! What an awful outsider!"

"Father said you wanted to meet him."

"Yes, I know. The fact is, you see, I want a bit, and the Major thinks he might part. I must be civil to him; the Major says I ought to take him to the club, and trot out a few dukes and that sort of thing. It seems beastly mean. It's

a hard world. But I wanted to talk to you. I 've
had a long jaw with Lucy, and it 's all right. Your
engagement, you know, and that. She sees what
a fool she made of herself, and she told me to
say she was sorry. Really, I 'm not humbug-
ging; it 's a proper apology; you know Jack
Ashton's wife 's a great pal of hers — "

" Ugh ! "

" Eh? Oh, she 's not a bad sort. Rather
jolly sort of woman. Good-looking, too; sport-
ing. Jack Ashton 's a decent sort of chap; selfish beggar, but — "

" Oh, never mind them."

" Well, anyhow it 's all right about Lucy.
You 'll forgive her, won't you? And, Nelly, I
want to say something seriously. I 'm infernally
sorry if I gave Lucy or anybody else any reason
to talk about us. It was stupid of us to go about
together so much; I never think of those things.
Now that you 're going to marry, I don't want to
spoil the show, you know. Not that — I did n't
mean to say anything conceited; you understand."

" Dear old Charlie, you 're awfully nice about
it. We 'll always be friends."

" Of course, dear. I wish I knew George

3

Ashton better. I suppose there's a lot of boodle. Rowe's an awfully nice place, they say —"

"Look here, Charlie; don't talk like that. You don't understand. Whatever Mildred Ashton or anybody may say, I'm not marrying George Ashton for Rowe, or to get a position, or that. Of course I'm glad to marry; I'm sick of this life; sick of home, sick of going about at a sort of disadvantage. I'm grateful to George Ashton, — you know I look things in the face, and I know how people talk about me, — I'm grateful to him, and I intend to do my share and be a decent wife to him. But I'd marry him anyhow. You and I are good friends, Charlie, but — but you see how it is."

"All right, old girl; that's straight. He's a lucky chap. As for people saying things, that's all rot. Anybody who's prettier and more popular than other people's sure to be talked about; you've always run straight, and you're going to run straight now. But Rowe isn't Victoria Road. They'll go on talking, but they won't say things to make you drop 'em when they get round to you. I suppose I've been a bad sort of friend to you. I don't think I'm worse than other people, but I'm more open, certainly; and they don't mince things when they talk about a chap who's been pongo and has n't a bob. Same with you in a way. You say things you don't mean, and repeat things you don't understand. I'm not much, I dare say; but you 've got more grit and more real goodness, by Jove, — "

" Eleanor," called Kate, " Mr. Morrison wants to hear you play."

So they went back to the drawing-room, where Nelly played, and Mr. Morrison gazed at her with heavy admiration, and Major Canover looked paternal, and Skeffington, who could have joked with a man who picked his pocket, became reserved and forgot the money he wanted.

And now I hope I have given some idea of the antecedents and characters of Nelly Canover and George Ashton, and how it came that they married one another, and of their friends' comments thereupon, and of what results might follow.

CHAPTER V

THE START

THEY were married in February, and started at once for Rowe. Old Mrs. Ashton remained in London; she was to follow them in a few days and to live in the Dower-house, — a course on which from the very first she had insisted.

In the rush of the weeks in London before the marriage there had been little chance that any firm relation — unless it had been one of hostility — should be formed between her and her daughter to be. Hostile to one another they certainly were not; that they were become fast friends could not be said. When George Ashton presented Nelly to his mother, the girl was nervous from sheer desire to please, and the older woman had intuition to perceive it; on both sides there was an intention to love. But an intention to love is not generally, so to speak, followed by an accomplishment; who say it may be will at least

allow that the schooling in love takes time. In
this case both in the bottom of their hearts fore-
told a difficulty, which would come from oppos-
ing antecedents and modes of thought. How
then could they love one another at sight ?
George Ashton, who sat in partial and unwise
silence during this first occasion of their meeting, was vaguely depressed in its progress. The
old-world breeding of his mother had not taught
her to affect effusive cordiality, beyond that
which in courtesy she gave to her own or a fellow guest. She was gentle and gracious to Nelly
Canover; she was not enthusiastic or embracing.
She was kind and open in her manner: she
feared, all things considered, that, were it protective, it might offend. On Nelly Canover the
effect was one of criticism, kindly criticism,
but criticism still. And she, who beyond the
trivial insincerities of every woman's life was
thoroughly and absolutely frank, from a sense of
their intimate relation, and it may be from a pro-
testing sense that there was nothing in her life to
give her shame, would not try to divine and pro-
pitiate the other's prejudices more than civility
required — as would many a woman, I think, of
whom the world speaks better than ever it spoke

of her.   Perhaps there are fewer women than
men who admire frankness for its own sake;
Mrs. Ashton was not one of them, and the impression that something alien was entering her
intimate life grew stronger as they talked.

"She's very pretty, George," she said afterwards, " — more than pretty; she is beautiful."

"You — you like her, mother?"

"We shall like one another all the more, dear,
for not jumping down one another's throats at
first.   You must not expect a clever girl who
lives in the world and an old recluse of a woman
to have every idea in common."

George sighed, and his mother gave him a
quick, half appealing look.

"I *do* like her, dear; I admire her very
much."

George kissed his mother, and they talked
of something else.

Jack Ashton had been hearty in his congratu-
lations, and so had been Mildred, his wife, but I
fear there was little reason in human nature why
she and Nelly Canover should love one another.
Nelly had ignored the past passage between
them with a sort of proud indifference to which
the other was not wholly insensible.   And Mrs.

Jack, who wished to be in a position of patronage towards the mistress of Rowe, and whose
method with objects of desire was to seize them
with a firm hand, was for once repulsed, not
with diplomacy, of which poor Nelly knew little,
but with a certain abruptness — deserved, it may
be, and the less likely to be forgotten. Of
George Ashton's friends Lady Tremayne was
gone to Ireland before he came to town, and
remained there in attendance on her husband,
who was ill of a returning ague. But Nelly
Canover found a fast friend in Mr. Wilmot, who
was charmed, delighted, impressed, and preached
her praises abroad.

"Don't despise old fellows," he had said to
her, on the occasion of some self-inspired chaff;
"people sometimes listen to their opinions, and
even a charming young lady may benefit by an
old fellow's good word." The kind light in his
eyes showed the sense of the speech, and Nelly
liked him.

"She's not only beautiful," he said to Mrs.
Ashton, "she's spirited and honest, and I never
met a better-bred girl in my life." To George
he said, "You're marrying the most charming
girl in England, my boy." George answered he

would try to be the best husband in England,
for his share. To which Mr. Wilmot replied,
" I hope you will, my dear fellow," with a
momentary seriousness. Large professions appeal to the humour of clever young men. " Ah,
Francis, we 're all angels," George said, " and
it 's a perfect world." And in spite of himself
Mr. Wilmot thought for a moment of George's
father.

There had not been very affectionate meet-
ings in Victoria Road. A prig and a nonentity,
as George Ashton and Kate Canover thought
one another, are not likely to be mutually
attentive. With Major Canover, George's
humour took a touch of the sardonic, and the
Major's geniality was some of the hardest work
in that well-spent life. It happened also that,
on his visits to Victoria Road, George frequently encountered Mr. Morrison, and conceived a pronounced dislike for that personage.
Thank God," he said once, as he left the
house, to Nelly in the hall, " you won't see any
more of that oily ruffian," and Nelly bit her lip.
Of Skeffington he remarked that he seemed a
good-hearted little chap, and Skeffington said of
him that he was a tremendously clever fellow.

And at last, after the jumble of all these encounters, Nelly Ashton was on her way to Rowe, leaving friends and enemies and neutral powers behind her. She had consented to go there willingly enough, to the surprise of her father and sister; she was glad to take her new life at once, to mark a revulsion from gaiety and Monte Carlo. Her husband wished it for a parallel reason; Rowe, with its rooms and trees and books, that were the symbols of his boyhood's stages, was aloof from his life in London, and the women therein, and now he was to take the one woman of the world to be a part of it, and his life thenceforth was to be straight and whole. (Acquit him of the prig's egotism; I but indicate an inarticulate feeling). There was another motive in their coming. George Ashton was not a rich man. His house was indeed a show-place, its park was large, and there was a fair shooting; but the land outside had been reduced by the sales of his predecessors to a small extent, and what there was brought him in but little money. He had inherited house property in the neighbouring town and money in the funds, some five thousand a year in all. But Rowe was an expensive

place to keep up, and if his wife was to have, as
he wished, a short season in town that year, they
could hardly go abroad now.   It was partly this
comparative scarcity of money (for the owner
of such a place) that had determined his long
sojourn at home.   And, by the way, the said
comparative scarcity had abated something
of the large-heartedness of Major Canover's
manner, who had imagined his son-in-law to
be about three times as rich as he was, and
who had suggested, in a generous way, such
settlements on his daughter as would have
involved the transference of the whole property
to her.   It never occurred to George to let his
place; he was a philosopher in theory and of a
rare conservatism in sundry practices; he was
Ashton of Rowe, which had never been let, and
where the reigning Ashton had always lived; he
smiled at the dignity, of course, in homage to
the inverted snobbishness of his time, which
affects to despise things not mean in a mean
way, but he would live at Rowe as his fathers
lived.

It was a cold evening when they arrived at
the little station.   They sat in silence during the
quick drive to the house, and Nelly, peering out

of the blurred windows of the brougham into the darkness, knew only that they were going through narrow, twisting lanes. She felt a faint tremor when she saw a dim figure courtesy as they went through the gates. As the brougham stopped, her husband pressed her hand, saying, " Welcome to your home, dear."

Standing at the foot of the broad steps she saw the house stretching dimly on either side of the light streaming from the door, and for a moment a sense of the unknown, the dangerous, came upon her. And then the housekeeper was welcoming her, and her new life was begun.

CHAPTER VI

NELLY ASHTON AT ROWE

I SHALL not essay to describe the tenderness of the first season of a marriage. " Cras amet qui nunquam amavit, quique amavit cras amet." It is good that there are times when individuality, and complexity, and waywardness, and the world are forgotten, and there is nothing to be recorded by a scribbler. George Ashton loved his wife after his fashion, and his wife imagined that she gave him all the love that was in her. They forgot themselves and the world for one another.

But by-and-bye, you know, as time goes on, oneself and the world will reassert themselves with more and more insistence. Husband and wife who live together must not only kiss but talk to one another, and in this was a certain difficulty. It was easy in London, when the language of love was temporarily forgotten, to

talk of people just met, and places just visited.
But there were not many people in whom both
were interested; their few neighbours suggested
but short remarks, and the emotions excited by
trees and grass do not make for garrulity. The
subjects of his larger interests recurred to George
Ashton; Nelly's thoughts began to wander to
scenes and people indifferent to him. He spent
longer hours in his library; she sometimes
knitted her brows in striving perplexity while
he talked. He had no sort of low pride in
superiority of knowledge, but he came to recognise that he must consider her capacity in conversation. Now it was a phrase of which the
allusion was lost, now a touch of humour
ignored. Spirit and honesty and generosity,
which his wife had, may shine in the play of
the world; they are of little use in a dual solitude in the country, where one rejoices mostly
in the pliability and reciprocity of ideas in which
she was to seek. Her beauty was before him;
but when a man who loves his library is coming
to think of his wife as a piece of beauty attached
to him — alack! Alack, at least, if he cannot be
a reasonable animal and take his pleasure sepa-
rately here and there. His enthusiasm was not

gone; he thought her still incomparable in his
experience, and that nothing really important
was amiss; but the wholeness of his ideal was
now diminished a little, and alack! for ideals
which are diminished.

Is there some air, some tune, or cadence,
which ever, when you chance to hear it, reminds
you, not of definite experiences, but of something vaguely fine and lost and regretted? If
it come amid the jarring noises of vulgar life, it
pains you; you wish it away; you would hear
it in solitude, at least in silence. Hearing such
a tune on the eve of his marriage George
Ashton would have taken it for a fitting accom-
paniment of triumph; hearing it now he would
have felt that there were things in life that he
had lost. And then, looking on his beautiful
wife, he would have worshipped her — for a
minute or two, until other thoughts came back
to him.

What would such a tune have said now to his
wife? She had been blithe and gay, taking the
moment absolutely, and to such natures reaction
comes heavily and of a sudden, opening a glimpse
of inarticulate pathos — and goes on a sudden
again. Meditation brings gloom to such lives as

these, and at Rowe there was occasion for Nelly Ashton to meditate. Save now and then, for some fleeting minutes, she was not happy. She missed more than she knew; there was present less than she had imagined.

There was the house and its environment. She admired it, and it was unfamiliar. Though it ranked among the most distinguished, it was not of the largest houses in its county; but it was, for her own, a very large house to Nelly. Except for occasional country visits, she had been accustomed to small rooms and a house which a voice could penetrate, and time is needed to render large rooms and general spaciousness, stateliness, and silence, friendly and comfortable. When she walked into the large drawing-room, or looked at the pictures in the gallery, she had a vague sense of acting a part and would go back to the little room she had made her own; going there she would come to the library, pause, and pass it. The servants and the management perplexed her. The housekeeper, who did not like her, worried her with questions; the French maid she had brought with her brought weeping complaints of the others; she was sure that money was wasted, and was as yet incompetent to save it.

The neighbours were a mild distress. She wished to please them for her husband's sake, and had, as I have said, but little diplomacy. The near neighbourhood was sparse; there was no occasion for the general distinction and superficial eminence and popularity which a girl of her beauty must have had in larger assemblies. The neighbours were few, and their favour required individual conciliation; and Nelly failed. Of course some of the men tried to flirt with her, and she, conscious of many innocent past flirtations, and overmuch on her guard, repelled them. The women were no more unamiable than the women of any other place. There was much of frank friendship and good comradeship among them, but these were the growth of intimacy and common interests; a necessary approach was through general topics, and on these Nelly Ashton and they came to deadlocks. She had none of their country interests. Those of them who lived at all in London society had acquaintances, at once less distinguished and more stable than hers, and the fact led inevitably now to jealousy, and now to superiority. They had little for conversation. For the place in which people live

and common acquaintances being ruled out,
what was there? Many of us know it for a fact
that the theatres are not an inexhaustible topic.
Mrs. Jack Ashton had written to some of her
friends, kindly bespeaking their patronage of the
new mistress of Rowe, and the tone of her good-
natured letters tended to an air of approach that
was quickly repulsed. Nelly Ashton, whose
beauty had made many men in love with her,
and whose honesty and loyalty had made some
her fast friends, felt a solitude among her neighbours in the country.

Already, then, the tune of her ideals, if she
had heard such a thing in the midst of her
neighbours, might not have made her long to be
alone with her husband — might have made her
think that her life in the past, the life of which
she had thought herself weary, had pleasant
spots in it for memory. And by some vague
association it might have brought to her mind a
little black-haired Irishman, with blue eyes and
a sweet smile, who had never failed to understand
her, and whom it was not hard to understand.

Between her husband's mother and her there
was perplexity. To the older woman this was
a dashing girl who had seen a great deal of the

world and must find the manipulation of Rowe
and its neighbourhood a bagatelle. She told
herself it was wise to leave the dower-house as
little as might be, that the best way to stand
well with her son's wife and keep her place in
her son's life was to avoid interference and
advice. She talked to Nelly of their neighbours, in a simple fashion, keeping much to the
facts; to advise her how to deal with this or
that one of them hardly occurred to her. Nelly,
on the other hand, would have welcomed Mrs.
Ashton's advice, and was distressed that it was
not given. She admired her manner sincerely.
"When I am old, George," she said once, "I
shall be very different from your mother.
Women like her are not made now." She
would have welcomed a kindly interest without
a touch of vanity. But it was not offered. She
was treated with studious equality, and she felt
as a result that she was on a trial and that to
court assistance was to confess defeat. "His
people hate our marriage, and want me to fail,"
she thought.

In this she was biased by the remembrance
of Mildred Ashton, her undisguised patronage,
and the look of amused toleration she had

adopted when repulsed. She had every possible right, she reflected, to resent the patronage of Mrs. Jack, who was worse born and worse bred than herself, and had treated her aforetime with calculated rudeness. And yet, she half con· fessed to herself, there was something in Mildred's imperturbable assurance and vigorous success which impressed her and almost made her afraid. She had dreamed one night that a boulder was slowly falling on her, that she pushed it back by a spirited effort two or three times, but that in the end it was pressing her to the earth, and, as she awoke, she saw somehow on the boulder the plump and smiling face of Mrs. Jack. She felt that this woman hated her and would show her no mercy if she tripped. And vaguely she felt that her husband's mother, more kind, would be even more critical, and was in a way on the side of the enemy.

And so two women who need have had no feeling in the world but kindness for one another stood apart for want of being drawn together. The one would have given her confidence, the other her counsel and help. If the one had said, " Mother, I am young, and this life is new to me; I want to please you and to be the wife you would wish for your son;" or if the other had said, "My daughter, I am an old woman, and have had a special experience; you must not be hurt if I try to make it of use to you;" then they would have embraced and been friends. But no such thing was said. The old woman, tender and lovable, thought with a sigh she was not needed; the girl, lovable and brave, thought she was left to stand alone. So her half helplessness, trivial in the scheme of things and accidental, oppressed her.

But she had her husband? Ah, yes, and, you know, they had married for love. Passionate love there had been on one side, self-convinced love there had been on the other.

They sat after dinner one night in the long low dining-room, with its oak and portraits and high-backed chairs, Nelly pale and a little tired, George meditative and slightly fidgeting. The butler, a thin old man, stooping and white-haired, had finished his rounds, and conversation, which had to be raised for the length of the flowered table, became more possible. It was six weeks after their marriage.

"Oh, George, I heard from Kate this afternoon."

"Yes? Quite well, I hope?" he looked up languidly.

"Oh, yes. She talks about coming down."

"Oh, well — it will cheer you up, dear."

"I don't want that. You don't mind her coming?"

"Why, of course not. I'm afraid it's rather a dull place for her, though."

"I—" began Nelly, but she looked embarrassed, and there was a pause. Then:

"Oh, and George, father wrote too. He — he wants me to lend him some money. I'm awfully sorry to bother you about it. He says something about a judgment summons—"

George laughed slightly, but quite without irritation.

"My dear girl, don't think it necessary to apologise. I daresay I'm often a bore, but I'm really not mean. If it gives you any pleasure to send the Major money, do by all means. Is it much?"

"Fifteen pounds. But I'm afraid I—"

"But you haven't any money in the bank. I'll give you a cheque to-morrow — to-night if you like. I can't pledge myself to the view that it will necessarily do the Major any good, but

of course, dear, you wish to help him. Will he
come down, by the way?"

"Kate says something about it. But if you 'd
rather — rather —"

"I don't know why you should seem to think
I want to be rude to your people. There 's nothing much for him to do, and as you know I 'm not
much good at amusing people. But I 'll do my
best."

"George, have I offended you?"

"No, no, dear — I 'm rather headachy, that 's
all — I think I read too long to-day. Only
please don't think I don't want to welcome
your people."

"No, George, I know."

She looked distressed. George drank a glass
of port, and filled another.

"By the way," he said, "there 's another offer
to mitigate our loneliness. Jack 's written sug-
gesting that, when we 've got over our honeymoon, as he kindly puts it, he and his wife
would like to come down for a few days."

Nelly looked up quickly and compressed her
lips.

"It 's nice of her to give me her *cachet*. Perhaps she might have written to me."

"Oh, my *dear* girl, *don't* talk like that. They're perfectly harmless, amiable people. They're easy to entertain: when they're not eating, they're cultivating their appetites. We won't have them if you don't like, but I think they might come for a few days."

"Oh, of course, George, that's all right."

There was another pause.

"Any one called to-day?" asked George.

"Only Mrs. Trenderham. She came when you'd gone out to walk."

"Frightful bore; why didn't she call before, though?"

"She said she'd been away. We — we didn't seem to have much to say to each other. — George, I'm not a success with your neighbours.'

"Oh, nonsense. Besides, if you weren't, what does it matter? I don't care two-pence about them. Of course, one or two are old friends of my mother's. They're fogies, most of them, but you'll like them well enough in time — "

"Mrs. Howlet" (the venerable housekeeper) "didn't like my arrangement of the drawing-room. I'm afraid I'm in her black books."

George was stirred for a moment.

"What infernal impertinence! If she does

that sort of thing she 'll have to go. You know she 's been here twenty years; it 's natural she should think the place belongs to her. But we shall have to pension her off or something. I 'll talk to her to-morrow."

" Oh, no, George, *please* don't. Of course it does n't matter. I only thought it would amuse you."

She smiled rather wearily, and rose to go. As her husband held the door for her, she turned her face to his, and he saw her big eyes were full of tears.

" My dearest, what is it ? I know, dear, you 're bored down here; it 's natural enough. We 'll go abroad for a bit; we 'll start to-morrow if you like."

" Oh, *no*, *no ;* I want to stay here; I want to love the place — I wish it would love me."

She looked at him appealingly and with a quivering mouth, and he swung the door back again and took her in his arms, and so — for a moment — any approach to quarrelling there had been was merged.

When she was gone, he walked about the room, his mouth slightly working, and looked now and again at a portrait and seemed to think.

Then he sat at the table and gradually finished
the bottle of port.

A fortnight later Kate and Major Canover
arrived. Their visit was not a triumph. Kate
thought the neighbours tedious, and was inclined
to talk London over their heads. The Major's
walks with his son-in-law became more and more
silent. Both he and Kate were disappointed in
the size of the place. Their call at the dower-
house began in geniality and ended in frigidity.
Neither Nelly nor George was sorry when they
left for town.

And after a month Mrs. Jack Ashton and her
husband descended upon Rowe. It was a far
more difficult thing for Nelly to resist her patronage here than in London. Mrs. Jack had made
two long visits before, and with vigorous interest
had gained a complete knowledge of the place,
and seemed to feel no delicacy whatever in
showing that it was superior to Nelly's. She
walked her hostess about the house and the
gardens, and stopped to ask the gardener about
his family, and to speak to the coachman's wife,
with whose domestic sorrows she was fully ac-
quainted. She was perfectly good-natured when

good nature cost her nothing, and was popular
with all these people. Nelly, a little thin now,
and fatigued, looked like a mere attendant on
the substantial and bustling Mrs. Jack, with her
air of kind-hearted proprietress.

George saw nothing of this. His cousin's
wife amused him; she talked to him gaily and
with deference for his book learning; it may be
that, dimly and unconsciously, her robust comeliness attracted him. She visited the dower-
house every day, and aired a sweetly affectionate respect for Mrs. Ashton, who was not a
cynic.

With the neighbours she was extremely popular. They all came to call on her; she remembered their affairs, and talked their talk. In
truth, Mrs. Jack Ashton was the star of that
district of Hampshire for a week, and it was one
of the most miserable in Nelly's short life. On
the last day of it there was a small dinner at
Rowe House, and Nelly felt it to be a climax.
She sat between a deaf old man and a middle-
aged admirer, rejected and sulky, and she heard
incessantly the cheerful tones of Mrs. Jack's
emphatic voice, and, whenever she looked up,
saw Mrs. Jack dispensing smiles and interested

glances.   However, on the next day Mrs. Jack returned to town, smiling to the last, and leaving regrets behind her.

And at length, in May, George Ashton and his wife went up to London for the season, each with a secret hope that what had been amiss at Rowe would there be righted.

CHAPTER VII

AN AFTERNOON IN TOWN.

GEORGE ASHTON had taken a little furnished house in Half-Moon Street. There was not much to arrange in it, and on the day after their arrival Nelly Ashton was at home, and sat in the small and prettily furnished drawing-room wondering if anybody would call. Lord Skeffington had written to her a week before, for the first time since her marriage, and she had told him of her plans in her answer. His letter was merely that of a simple correspondent, relating the bald facts of his movements, asking her how she was, lamenting finally the loss of her society. She had begun, as you have read, to think somewhat wistfully of Skeffington, of the unreflecting good fellowship and the unquestioned pleasures the idea of him recalled. She thought so of him now, as she looked out on the street and smelt the mental atmosphere of London — that sense

of familiar business or idleness renewed, of throng-
ing associations, and of sympathetic humanity,
which comes so gratefully to country-wearied
cockneys. Ah, the country and the new shel-
tered life, and the higher plane, and rarified
joys, and seemly traditions! And ah, the
dinners and theatres and flirting looks and whisk-
ing hansom cabs! And ah, poor Nelly Canover
who was, who had been wearied of these
symbols, so full of sacred expectancy! She
drummed on the carpet with her foot, she kept
time to a street organ. Dear old Charlie Skeffington, how delightful to see him again! Of
course he was not an equal of her husband, but it
is pleasant to see old friends. Perhaps he would
call that afternoon.

She wondered if anybody else would. Her
father, perhaps, and Kate. Possibly Mildred
Ashton, to a friend of whom the house in Half-
Moon Street belonged, and who therefore knew of
the arrival, and would be sure to come presently
to inspect and to patronise. Nelly glanced half
nervously round as she thought of it, and then
thought how absurd she was. It was so idiotic
to feel a dim rivalry between herself and Mrs.
Jack, so utterly idiotic to feel dimly afraid of her.

Why should she be hated, and how could she be
injured by this woman? It was absurd. And
yet she knew that she was hated, and felt vaguely
that she must stir herself to fight against injury.
She felt the discomfort of the weaker will. There
was something strong in Mildred Ashton, something that seemed to bear her down. She owned
to herself that in Hampshire she had not in the
end resisted the other's patronage, had suffered
herself to be treated as an object of superior
good-nature, and as she owned it she stamped
with irritation. In what conceivable point was
she Mildred's inferior? She walked to a glass
and looked on a face of perfect, romantic beauty.
In what conceivable manner could she be over-
come by Mrs. Jack, with her commonplace,
coarse good looks (so she honestly thought
them), with her loud laugh and pushing air?
She sat down in frowning thought. Of course,
if she had a son, Jack Ashton and his wife or
their child would not have Rowe, and for such a
reason as that Mrs. Jack, who had a reputation
for hearty good-nature, hated her — how pitiably
mean! And here Nelly's mouth puckered, and
she looked very sad. Perhaps her beauty was
the cause, — how vilely contemptible!

In spite of woman's vanity, it is a fact that she did not fancy that her own fineness of nature and essential delicacy which the commoner and shrewder woman roughly perceived were a further motive, equal at least to her beauty, and that the patronage and self-assertion were to such a woman a necessary consequence. She would not think about it, but with the effort to send it from her mind there rose the more clearly the image of Mrs. Jack Ashton, smiling and prosperous, waiting for an opportunity to injure her, strong and merciless to use it. The unsuccess on which she had brooded had touched her nerves, and she gave a gesture of despair — the despair of the brave who do not know where to strike in defence.

Lord Skeffington saw it as he followed the servant into the room. Nelly, who was sitting with her back to the door, jumped up and held out her hands. "Oh, Charlie, how jolly to see you."

"Well, dear, glad to see your old pal?" He had intended to recognise the new position of things by a more formal mode of address; but friends are friends, and Irish Irish. "By Jove, Nelly, it seems a thousand years since I saw you. How are you? Let me look. H'm — my dear, you're pale, and you look tired. The journey, I suppose. But the country ought to have done you more good than that. You're thinner —"

"Oh, never mind me. I am longing to hear about you — about everything. Who was at Monte? Your letter only repeated the postmark over again. All the old set?"

"Oh, yes, rather a clipping time on the whole. Poor old Billy had a new system, and it was the greatest joke in the world to see him and little what's-her-name — you know —"

And so they talked the old talk, the talk of innocent, irresponsible worldlings, and Nelly's eyes grew brighter as she renewed the good time when she was so miserable. Here was no puzzling for a meaning, no wrong construction one could not explain. She laughed freely, and everything seemed indifferent and amusing. But by-and-bye Skeffington, who was no egotist, insisted on hearing of her life in the country. He put his questions with a grave appreciation, without a sign of the appalling boredom the answers suggested to him, and Nelly therefore could the more easily indicate, without consciousness of disloyalty, that all her way had not been roses.

But she did not go far. The most was, " Charlie, I feel rather as if I 'd not given satisfaction, don't you know — to the place, of course, I mean. I 'm not cut out for the sort of thing. I hoped I should be able to — but I 'm afraid — I don't know."

" Oh, nonsense ; you 'll take to it all right in time. When I was young — well, when I came over from Ireland for the first time to go to Eton — I daresay I did n't seem cut out for a life of bankruptcy and dissipation." He gave his pleasant little laugh. "But I 've got on very well at it all the same."

" Poor old Charlie, I think there 's a fate against us both. We ought to be pals."

At this point there was heard a resolute knock at the hall door, and Nelly's gaiety suddenly forsook her. " Oh, I do believe that 's Mildred Ashton."

"That 's Jack Ashton's wife, is n't it? Jolly woman, I always thought her."

" Oh ! — she 's — she 's — we shall never be friends."

Skeffington smiled a smile of that toleration with which men hear of feminine animosities. " You 're different styles, certainly," he said.

5

It was indeed Mrs. Jack who sailed into the room with a loud and cheerful greeting. Skeffington, observing the kindness of her manner towards Nelly, was confirmed in his opinion of her good-nature.

"I hoped I should be the first to come to you," she said. "But Lord Skeffington has beaten me. How are you?" turning to him, "and how's my dear Lucy?"

"Oh, all right, thanks; she couldn't come with me to-day because she had to go to her mother."

"I see, and you couldn't wait," said Mrs. Jack with a faint smile, as she settled herself comfortably and, observing the entrance of tea, took off her gloves. There was silence for a moment, and she kept her eyes on her white and much-ringed hands.

"Yes, please, dear; lots of cream and two lumps of sugar. Rowe looking as lovely as ever?" She began a series of questions about the country, to which Nelly replied rather nervously, whilst Skeffington, feeling bored, handed cups and things, and listened.

"Is Mrs. Ashton coming to town at all?"

"Yes, in a few days. She's going to present me on my marriage, you know."

"Oh, I'm *so* glad," said Mrs. Jack, and Nelly bit her lip, and had no rejoinder to Mrs. Jack's quite superfluous gladness.

"Have you been presented before? No? Well, if you want any tips I shall be glad to coach you."

She herself had barely emerged from her chrysalis at Highgate at the time of her marriage, and had been presented for the first time by Mrs. Ashton, but the fact did not disturb her complacent superiority in the least. Again, to rejoin was to assume a rather vulgar level of social ambition. Skeffington saw nothing in the remark but a reasonable kindness in an unimportant matter. Mrs. Jack's air of success was intensified.

Presently Skeffington took his leave, and she said good-bye to him with something in her manner of the cold finality of a displeased chaperon, which he did not notice, but which Nelly perceiving coloured.

She made her own manner the friendlier in consequence.

"Good-bye, Charlie ; come again soon. You must come and dine, and Lady Skeffington, if she will."

When the door closed behind him, Mrs. Jack looked at Nelly with eyebrows slightly, but perceptibly, raised.

"Poor Lord Skeffington! What a pity he's so wild."

"I never heard of his doing any harm to a soul."

"Oh, no, of course not. Still he *is* wild, isn't he? What silly people call a dangerous man. You know Lucy Skeffington's one of my greatest friends. Poor dear. Thanks, I'll have another cup. Don't get up. Oh, thanks. It's frightfully greedy, but I'll have some more cake."

As Nelly stood in front of her with the cake she looked up at her smiling and said with deliberation: "Now, tell me honestly, did you find your life at Rowe everything you expected?"

Nellie looked down at the plump inquisitor. She believed the intention was impertinence, but the tone and the look were kind.

"Thank you, everything," she said, and went back to her seat a little abruptly.

"Well, that's all right. You see, dear, I've married an Ashton myself; so I can talk about it, can't I? They're all delightful, of course,

but you know they're full of old-fashioned
prejudices.   Some of Jack's ideas are ridiculous.
They don't understand new customs at all.   One
has to be old-fashioned about some things.   I
have n't offended you?"

"Why should you have?"

"That's right. You know what I mean.
Old Mrs. Ashton and I have great confidences.
She's an old dear, but in some things she
belongs to centuries ago. People like our
friend Lord Skeffington would frighten her
dreadfully."   She laughed and concentrated
her attention on her slice of cake.

"I don't think I quite understand what you
mean."

"Only that I think we must study those kind
of prejudices, must n't we? You see, I've had
some experience of the family, and I thought
it would be kind to give you the benefit of it.
I only meant in a general way, of course. I
should like to do anything I can for you."

"It's very good of you, but about—"

"Oh, not at all," interrupted Mrs. Jack
hastily; "but I must be moving on. One must
make the most of a day like this in town,
must n't one?"   She bustled and gave Nelly no

opportunity to speak. "*Good*-bye, dear; come
and see me soon."   She held out her hand, and
Nelly, as she took it, felt that it had struck her.
So in a cloud of benevolence and affability Mrs.
Jack departed.   Nelly walked to the window
and looked out despairingly.   She watched Mrs.
Jack get into her smart victoria, who looked up
and waved her hand.   Nelly did not smile back,
and Mildred, seeing the sorrowful face, drove
away radiant, as one who in a virtuous manner
enjoyed a victory.

Coming in a few minutes later, George Ashton
found his wife still standing at the window.
"Mildred's been here," she said.

"I know, I saw her in the street and she
stopped to speak.   Sorry I was out."

"Do you like her, George?"

"Oh, yes, pretty well.   She's a very good-
natured woman."

"*Is* she?"

"Oh, yes, I'm sure she is.   I know you don't
like her; I wish you did, rather.   I've never
seen anything in her manner that isn't perfectly
friendly, and my mother approves of her.   I
don't suppose she's particularly delicate or sensitive and that sort of thing.   That's largely a

question of brains. Still, she means well;
she's a very good wife and mother and all
that. Not particularly cogent reasons for de-
lighting in her society, perhaps, but I really
can't see how she's offensive."

"All right, George; I daresay I'm foolish
about her. — George, do you object to my
friendship with Charlie Skeffington?"

George put down his cup gravely. "Object?
You talk as if I were a Turk. You are the best
judge of what society pleases you."

The remark was enlightened, and yet somehow
it seemed to give no extraordinary pleasure to
his wife.

"Mildred suggested —"

"Oh, I see, I see. It was very stupid of her.
But upon my word, Nelly, I think she meant it
kindly. It was the sort of blundering kindness
that annoys one more than anything, but I think
one ought to forgive it. As for Skeffington, I
don't think he's exactly intellectual, but I'm
not a prig about that. I never heard anything
against him except ordinary dissipation, and I
don't care two-pence about that either. Has
he been here to-day? Sorry I missed him.
What shall we do to-night? Anything?"

" I should like to go to a theatre, I think."

" Oh, is there anything on that won't bore one to death ? "

" Oh, we won't go if it bores you. I like the lights and things. But we won't go; I don't care what we do."

" Oh, yes, we may as well do that as anything. Will you look something out and send down for seats? I must finish something I was writing before dinner."

He left the room, and Nelly looked up a theatre without interest and sent for seats, and stood again at the window looking out. London had not begun very brilliantly, she thought.

CHAPTER VIII

MR. MORRISON

"IT's not a very great favour to grant your old father. I've worked hard enough for you, my girl."

Major Canover was quite in earnest, but, like many people of shallow emotions, was unable to express many of them except in the unconsciously assimilated methods of the theatre. His daughter Nelly, perhaps from custom, did not doubt his sincerity. They were both troubled, he from genuine anxiety and annoyance that a trivial request should be refused, and she because good nature and wisdom said different things. The request was merely that Nelly should accompany him and her sister to dinner with Mr. Morrison and afterwards to a theatre. Her husband was gone into the country for a night, and she had no engagement.

" Why on earth you can't do a simple thing

like this I can't conceive. You don't dislike
him yourself, do you?"

I am afraid it was a fact that she did not dislike Mr. Morrison. I have indicated the atmosphere in which she had lived, one in which it
seemed that to be of expensive habits was the
first attribute of a male. Mr. Morrison had this
attribute. I have heard it said that if a man is
commonly polite in his manners he may pass
with many women for a gentleman. Mr. Morrison was elaborately polite. Admiration is
displeasing to few of us, and Mr. Morrison's
admiration was not hidden. And it is possible
to be the reverse of vulgar in grain and yet not
to escape at once the superficial effects of a
vulgar environment.

"No, I don't, but George hates him."

The Major smothered a manly execration.
"It's not fair to your husband," he said, and
the brilliancy of his diplomacy restored his
self-satisfaction, "to treat him as though he were
a domestic tyrant. God bless my soul! If a
man's going to forbid his wife to speak to her
father's friends just because he does n't happen
to like them himself, why, she might just as well
be a slave. No, no, you do George an injustice.

He does n't happen to like Morrison, who 's a
very good fellow, and a rich fellow, mind you,
and a man who 's done me a service — we all
have our fads about people. But as for object-
ing to your going with your own father and
sister to dine with him, why— "

The Major's hands made a gesture of universal
generosity and toleration.

" Father, why should Mr. Morrison be so
anxious I should come? "

" Why? why not? He likes you, I suppose,
and admires you, in a respectful sort of way —
an intellectual admiration." He pronounced
the phrase with satisfaction and perhaps did not
see in his mind the admirer's heavy sallow face,
thick lips, and beady eyes.

" You see, my dear," he continued, " all it
amounts to is, that Morrison has obliged me,
and in return I want to make up a pleasant
little party for him, and the best way to do so is
to get you to come. He 'll give us an excellent
dinner, and I suppose he 's taken a box somewhere. I 'm sure you won't refuse your old
father such a little thing as that? I only want
to return Morrison's kindness by giving him a
little gaiety. Poor fellow, he does n't get much;

does n't know many people, in fact. Well, that's settled, is n't it? We 'll call for you at half-past seven."

"Oh, all right, father; it 's not worth making a fuss about."

The Major went away at once as a wise man.

It was a month since Nelly and her husband were come to town, a month full of enjoyment for neither of them. George was dissatisfied. The facile pleasures of a stray man had ceased for him, partly as a direct result of his marriage, and partly because his early love for his wife had raised a desire for deeper, finer, and more pervading emotions than these facile pleasures do generally comprise. Some of them were left of necessity, for George Ashton had been married but a few months, and was neither a Mohammedan nor a brute; and others — the little fleeting, innocent games of half-love for example — were not for his serious mood. I hope you will not think him a prig when I tell you that in this period the ordinary funny story of masculine conversation jarred upon him. He was still, you see, in the face of an ideal, still on a spiritual plane above the common things: it was only that the ideal grew dim and receded

and was leaving him hopeless. He could not
set himself to study; his books were at Rowe,
his little den in Half-Moon Street suggested
anything but a proper use of brains. The
general run of his friends — as sometimes happens with men of intellectual bent and fastidious
tastes — was not intellectual, and cards and
sauntering and stories bored him now. His
wife's contingent irritated him. There were
professionally clever people who had written
books he disliked; there were men of florid
habit and experiences trivially cosmopolitan;
there were women who sometimes gushed and
sometimes joyed in pointless impropriety. He
liked best of them all a few irresponsible, well-
bred, and foolish young men, who chaffed with
Nelly and could be amiably rude, but he did
not invariably contrive to be amused by them.
The position of wet blanket in his own drawing-
room was terrifying to a sensitive humour, and
he betook himself frequently to his club. And
there a taste of which no state of our intellects
or affections can deprive us came to his rescue,
and older men consulted his judgment of wine.
It was surely an opportunity for a good influence. He wrote a few abstract letters to

Lady Tremayne.   But she was still in Ireland.
One doubts, however, if, at thirty, the influence
on a man of such a woman is so potent as it is
known of all men to be at twenty.   One thinks
perhaps that a girl, good, gay, clever, and un-
tempered by experience — a girl to make cynics
blush and misogynists hide their heads — might
have been a star to him.   Nelly Canover had
been his star, and somehow, when he had taken
and fitted it to a household lamp, the light
which had burned so brightly seemed to lan-
guish, and there was a little smoke or so about
the edges.   Give him your pity.

And Nelly the while was dissatisfied — with a
dissatisfaction the deeper for a vague self-blame
which did not occur to the lord of creation.
The displeasure with many of her friends which
she discovered in her husband was incompre-
hensible to her.   Of old, when Skeffington or
another had objected to this or that man, that
he was an " outsider," she had referred their
criticism to masculine vanity and rivalry, and
laughed.   Being conscious now that she gave
her husband no ghost of a reason for jealousy,
she did not understand his objections.   " A man
does not make himself a gentleman by keeping

a private cab and spending two pounds on his dinner," he had said, and Nelly's sharp "of course not" conveyed a suspicion that the undeniable assertion had been put fallaciously. "I don't see that the social qualification of a cad is improved by his having written a caddish book." "He's frightfully clever;" "Which makes him more ingeniously maddening." "Oh, dear; oh, dear!"

Skeffington and others had refrained from criticising the women of her friends. With a few of them her husband seemed to be in some sort of accord. But once, when two of them had left them, he said, "Are they very great friends of yours?" "Oh, no, they're all right, but I don't care about them." "Then I propose to make a general remark; one of your clever friends might make an epigram out of it. Bad morals are not a sufficient apology for bad manners," and he left the room.

It must be confessed that, though his toleration for antipathetic presences in his house was extreme, his method, when he came to objection, was not the most agreeable to a down-right nature. The method was, I think, to be condemned; what social sages would say of the

toleration, I do not know. Perhaps there are
women of immemorial traditions who would be
embarrassed by the latter procedure; against
the former it is certain Nelly's spirit rose. "He
tells me to gratify myself about people, and I
naturally see my old friends, and then he says
unpleasant things about them." At first she
took heed to his objections; she was coming
now to study a disregard of them. There was
one man about whom he had lost his temper
from the first, and that man was the respectable
Mr. Morrison. "I know nothing against him,"
he had said, "but his appearance and his conversation, and that is enough. He has brute and
blackguard written all over him, and his talk's
like a stream of bad oil. If he comes into the
house, I'll have any piece of furniture he touches
thrown out of window." Nelly laughed at this
display. It did not make her colour as other of
her husband's criticisms, and she had not invited
Mr. Morrison to Half-Moon Street. And now
at the end of the month she was going to dine
with Mr. Morrison. You see her spirit had
risen.

The dinner was largely elaborate, and the
host, perhaps from an artistic sense of a fitting

atmosphere, talked throughout of his magnifi-
cence. The Canovers and Nelly were privileged to hear of his yacht, his carriages — he
had not much to say of his horses — and the
expensive sources of his cellar. He related
these things with beady glances towards Nelly,
with the air of a conqueror, as Achilles may
have shown his muscles to Briseïs. I wish I
could say that the complaisance of his hearers
was an effect of breeding alone.

They went after dinner to a theatre, where Mr.
Morrison was sufficiently confident in himself to
keep his eyes fixed upon Nelly's profile. " See
Nelly Canover, — beg her pardon, — Ashton ? "
said a young man in the stalls to his companion.
" Prettier than ever. Shall we go round after
this ? " " Don't feel very keen. Never cared
much about the sister or the Major — that is
him, is n't it ? Besides, there 's a most awful
monster man with them. Who is he ? " " Don't
know; probably some wealthy beast the
Major 's got in tow. I say, though, what sort
of fellow 's this Ashton chap she 's married ? "

" Decent chap, I believe, a gentleman, and
that sort of thing." " He must be a fool then to
let his wife be trotted about by her awful dad."

"Oh, one never knows," — the joys of the youthful cynic! — "Daresay he's got some game of his own."

Certainly the presence of Mr. Morrison, — the large and magnificent, — while it might inspire awe in the insolvent, did not bring on his friends a halo of reverence or even aristocracy. Major Canover sighed with relief as he went out of the box between the acts, leaving Mr. Morrison to talk to Nelly in what he honestly believed to be a seductive manner, and Kate to sit in silence and sulky boredom. And poor Nelly, conscious at last of the man's vulgarity, and of a wrong position for herself, became very unhappy.

"Now for supper," said Mr. Morrison, when the play was over.

The Major beamed on the younger people's enjoyment, but Nelly managed to escape and betook herself home alone.

She was sitting the following afternoon alone in the little drawing-room, cross with herself and crosser, as was proper, with the perversity of things, when Mr. Morrison called, illustrating the terrible power which the pushing and coarse-grained have (did they know it) over their more amiable fellow-creatures.

" I hope I 'm welcome," said the large man as he came into the room, smiling hideously, and with the air of a self-made sultan.

Now, if Nelly Ashton had been a coster-girl or a great lady of the popular imagination, she would have had no difficulty in expressing that he was not welcome. As it was, she was almost helpless to convey this fact to Mr. Morrison's intelligence; he probably took her coldness for a natural awe of the powerful and conquering male. There used to be a story of a very young man in the army who, having bored his colonel's wife almost to death for an hour, and being invited, in despairing hope of variety, to walk in the garden, announced in so many words that he made it a rule never to flirt with the wives of his brother officers. Mr. Morrison would have missed the story's point.

But the interview was mercifully short, for Mr. Morrison, a man of simple ideas, sat down at once by her side on the sofa and tried to take her hand.

" You seem to be confusing me with someone else."

" Oh, no, I 'm not," — the insinuation had no doubt at all, — " you 're yourself, you know."

She had moved to another seat and the man stood up and put his hands in his pockets.

"Look here," he said, "your father and I have had dealings together."

He was triumphantly proof against the look which is supposed to crush anybody.

"Dealings together, and we may have more. The advantage has been on his side," with an omnipotent gesture, "and may be more so. That being the case, I may ask for a little kindness from you. Just a little kindness."

And so the interview came to an end, for even Mr. Morrison was wise enough not to wait until the bell was answered. He flushed as he went, and I think the anger in his face was less offensive than the preceding anticipation. All the same it is a pity that, when a proposal was recently advanced for clothing the Mr. Morrisons of London in a distinctive dress, the objections were found insuperable.

Nelly stamped her foot when he was gone, and sat down to write to her much-tried father. The only consolation was pleasure in her husband's justification, which she was glad to recognise. He had been right about this man; perhaps he was not altogether wrong about

others. You see what manner of wife she was
or might have been, one who needs convincing,
one who is glad to be convinced. Suppose a
definite, unerring line in a husband: there will
be thunder and lightning, and afterwards peace
and the smell of the sweet evening. Suppose
reason, tolerance, disapproval ironically suggested, and occasional sharp speech, and you
have the day ending in drizzle, the night clos-
ing hopelessly. And yet reason is all our boast,
and delicacy of conduct, as George Ashton said,
largely a matter of brains. It seems that tolerance and freedom make marvellously for happiness in marriage, when wife and husband have
the same tastes and like temperaments. Or
sensible men and women of the world go their
ways and are friends. Nelly Ashton was a girl
of spirit, and one unformed, and her husband
thought well to stand apart and criticise. Alas
for poor reason! Nelly Ashton could not understand its blessing.

She intended now to tell her husband — who
was to return that afternoon — of her ill chance
with Mr. Morrison, knowing him above a vulgar
misinterpretation, and to form that little bond of
common execration. I suppose that would have
been dull for the humorous gods.

For it happened that George Ashton's cab was three doors from his house in Half-Moon Street as Mr. Morrison left it. George had spent the evening before in long talk with his mother, renewing something of his boyhood, expressing vaguely an unhappiness, and receiving, as always, comfort and a stimulus to put himself in harmony with the world. His mother had talked gently to him of girls and their ways, their ideals and their mistakes, and of what they value in men — talked perhaps with a wise hypocrisy and hoping little, for she did not think that the girlhood of which she thought so wistfully and kindly was that of her son's wife. He was thinking now of Nelly with a sort of tender humour, which was his real possibility of wisdom, and which, if the chances of life had helped it, might have made a woman happy. When he saw Mr. Morrison, he cut him without hesitation, and, entering his house, went quickly to the drawing-room.

"Were you at home to that man Morrison?"

"Yes, that is, I didn't ask him to call. He was simply shown up."

"I see, but I don't quite understand how even a cad like that could have the impertinence to

call here — have you been meeting him at your
father's?"

"Been meeting him? My dear boy, you talk
as though I'd been making rendez-vous with
Mr. Morrison."

"No, but why should he think he might come
here?"

"Really, George, are we playing at witness
and lawyer? As a matter of fact, I dined with
Mr. Morrison last night."

She had flushed slightly and stood upright by
the fireplace. Her husband sat down and looked
at her coldly.

"Indeed? if it's not being too inquisitive,
may I ask who the rest of the party were?"

"Father and Kate."

"How delightful! You didn't mention the
engagement; I should have felt less rude in
leaving you alone if you had. Mr. Morrison
must be a charming host. I'm afraid I was
barbarian enough to cut him just now. If I'd
known of his hospitality, I'd have stopped and
thanked him."

"You mean, I suppose, I am not to know
my father's friends. I wish you'd speak
plainly."

"Not at all. I don't think I have tried to make you give up Major Canover's agreeable friends. I believe I speak ordinary English."

She gave a gesture of irritation. "I'm sorry you're angry with me, but I see nothing I should apologise for."

"It's I who should apologise for catechising you — "

"Will you excuse me? I've rather a headache. We shall meet at dinner, I suppose."

To be cut short in a strain of irony annoys the vanity of sarcastic people. George Ashton may have felt dimly that he deserved it, but he opened the door with a politely indifferent intimation of his sorrow for his wife's headache, and on this occasion there was no embrace to end the quarrel.

CHAPTER IX

A HOUSE PARTY AT ROWE

AFTER the incident of Mr. Morrison, George Ashton and his wife grew in politeness to one another. So would not (you will think) two healthy human natures. Your simple and healthy natures who are newly married may fall out, but in the inevitable course of married life are quickly friends again. An agricultural labourer and his wife, who are supposed to be naturally straightforward, — there is, I have observed, some evidence against the invariable truth of the supposition, — might fight and kiss again; would hardly maintain reserves and distances. Jack Ashton could not have lived with a woman but on terms of easy openness; Mildred, his wife, had her husband been distantly polite to her, would have bullied him into submission or have thrown herself at his feet as their relative forces or the chances of war determined. And who denies

that on the highest tower of our brain-built
castle of humanity — out of ken of Jack Ashton
and his wife — there may stand men and women
who are sound and whole in spirit and body, who
living together could not be other than frank and
direct and therefore friends in body and spirit?
Who knowing them is not glad the poor world
contains them? Who not being of them but regrets — regrets, if he is right, that he has paid in
perversity for subtlety and brains to which they
were free-born?

But I am writing of a man to whom had come
through his fathers with a body only tolerably
sound a spirit which was perverse. He had
pondered and analysed and examined; he was
fastidious; a rebuff to his mind and his tastes
tended to cool his passions. That he was worthy
of his wife I do not say. And yet he was honourable and generous, incapable of lying for advantage or of telling the truth for revenge. He
had plenty of humour; the ridiculous element in
his present position was quite apparent to him.
But he could not break through the barrier of
distaste which kept him there. If his wife had
committed a murder — so it was not a mean
murder — he would not have assumed even an

air of forgiveness. But when his wife showed a
liking for vulgar people, and misinterpreted
himself, he grew polite.

Nelly on her part found what she took to be
her patience breaking down. She was curt to
him at times; she consulted him less and less in
her engagements. She imitated his politeness,
and the necessity (as she thought it) irritated
her natural frankness; there was growing in her,
because of it, a feeling which she did not know
to be contempt. She was sounder in spirit than
her husband, but she was not wholly sound. An
appeal to her frankness and honesty would always
have found an answer, but failing that she was
liable to imaginings and suspicions. She saw
one day Mildred Ashton look compassionately
upon her husband; at once she thought he had
spoken of her to this woman, and the feeling
which she did not know to be contempt waxed
stronger.

They went abroad after London, and in an
hotel, where were friends of theirs, politeness
was easier than in Half-Moon Street. The
friends were Lord and Lady Skeffington. Skeffington was glad to be with his pal, as he called
her; Lady Skeffington was said by gossip, with

which you and I have nothing to do, to have followed in the wake of a pal of her own. She and Nelly were now on tolerable terms. I do not know that it is necessary we should assume that Lady Skeffington was wildly devoted to her lord or wildly jealous on his behalf. She was the daughter of a country doctor, brought up in an atmosphere not very ethereal, and she had married Charles FitzHenry, Viscount Skeffington in the peerage of Ireland, with, we will say, the laudable object of reclaiming and making him respectable with her father's savings. She had thought in the old days that his friendship with Nelly Canover was making herself ridiculous. Perhaps there were other reasons for hostility; now it had passed away, and probably Nelly and she really thought they were friends.

George looked with eyes of equable boredom on everybody but his wife, for cooled passion may be thought a different thing. But he liked Skeffington, who would crack a bottle at any reasonable time (in an immemorial fashion whose decease was falsely announced in the papers a while ago) and play picquet for any reasonable number of hours. You really cannot introspect all day and night.

In the beginning of September they returned to Rowe. Mrs. Ashton welcomed them with a look of anxiety which neither could altogether miss. George, being a man, put it down to fears for his happiness and laughed as he kissed his mother. Nelly, being a woman, knew what was wanting. I cannot tell what she thought, but at least a child would have drawn these two women together.

A day or two after their arrival George went to London on business and returned with a bracelet for his wife.

"Oh, George, how lovely; thank you so much." "Dear" was half formed on her lips, and there was a look in her eyes which a man should have seen.

George was not looking at her. "So glad you like it: I thought it was pretty."

"Thank you so very much."

"Not at all," he said with the little laugh she did not understand. After all it would have been sordid to have been reconciled by means of a bracelet.

The next day came a letter from Mildred Ashton remarking that it would be so sweet if Nelly could take in for a week herself and her husband and the baby, for whom it seemed there was no other occasion to obtain fresh air. A few months back Nelly might have expressed vexation, before she and her husband were grown polite.

"It won't bore you?" he asked.

"Oh, not at all. But it would be dull for them alone. Would it bore you if I asked the Skeffingtons down? I know they are free now."

Nelly, you see, had thought of Skeffington at once as a counterpoise to her enemy, with much nature and little prescience.

"Delighted. The birds aren't much this year, but I daresay Skeffington won't mind getting his hand in with them."

"Oh, Charlie won't mind that."

"No? that's all right then." He did not raise his eyebrows.

So Lord and Lady Skeffington were invited and came to Rowe, and thus it happened that three married couples were assembled to example possibilities — the Jack Ashtons affectionate and contented, the Skeffingtons good-humoured and indifferent, George and Nelly Ashton as you have seen them. The Skeffington children, who were two, took the fresh air in Ireland with their grandmother.

The Jack Ashtons came first, and on the afternoon of their arrival the baby, his mother, his nurse, and his hostess went down to the dower-house. Mrs. Ashton was devoted to children and lavished caresses on the healthy little boy for his own sake.   If she was wistful, she did not show it ; if Mrs. Jack was triumphant, surely the existence of the baby was excuse enough. Nelly, standing aside, thought such thoughts as no man knows.

When the Skeffingtons came, the party was outwardly amused.   All six had the modern habit of inoffensive chaff, inoffensive, at least, when chaffers and chaffees (they especially) are tolerably amiable, the chaff which, whatever the elders say against it, is the easiest and most pleasant substitute for intimacy or reasoned conversation.   Inwardly there were varieties of view.   George Ashton was bored and annoyed. The society of the amiably vacuous can be endured for a longer time than that of the agressively intelligent, but in either case the longing for reaction may grow painful. Lady Skeffington was socially clever and could appear to be irresponsible. She responded gaily to her host ; now and again she told a funny story ; when

dullness threatened too visibly, she produced a
South-Cork brogue.   But George Ashton would
not flirt with her, and Jack Ashton's flirting was
not desirable of lively woman; Lady Skeffington was bored to desperation.   Nelly was the
most silent of them all, and lapsed most frequently from smiles.   The presence of Mildred oppressed her;   the daily eulogies on the baby
were a torture.   Skeffington paired off with
her as often as was possible, but he did not
bring her the comfort she had expected.   A
life such as his does not sharpen the sensibili-
ties.   He was fond of Nelly, and gay in her
society, and he was honest in thinking that, if
need were, he would stand her firm friend.   But
the nature of her perplexities escaped him.   He
thought George Ashton a good enough fellow,
a bit of a prig perhaps, but really a very decent
chap; Nelly had come, really, into rather a
good thing; you can't have everything you
want, and Nelly had enough to satisfy most
people.   He laughed at her vague animadver-
sions on Mildred Ashton, whom he thought a
very good-natured and easy-mannered person.
Women's quarrels amused him.   The Mohammedan view of their souls, if he had ever thought

of souls, would have seemed tenable to him.
They quarrelled, he thought, for the pettiest
reasons, and were reconciled for the like. And
in this case the quarrelling seemed to be all on
one side. He was not then a very sympathetic
listener. And perhaps he was accustomed to
Nelly's beauty; he showed no intention of
grave advances. Nelly was unhappy. There
was a man who had disappointed her hopes of
herself, a man who was an ox, and a man who
did not understand as once he had under-
stood; and there were two women who watched
her.

But this unfortunate trio was balanced. Skeffington was happy. The house was charming,
its habits such as were familiar. Everybody
was agreeable, and he had his old pal with whom
to stroll about. The shooting was not good,
but it filled up a few hours every day and kept
him fit. In a more bovine fashion Jack Ashton's feelings were the same. The food was
good, and the wine was good, and he had that
consciousness of leading a healthy life which
was the highest gratification of his moral sense.
He regarded Lady Skeffington as a sort of sherry
and bitters before dinner, a sort of liqueur

afterwards, and he took for granted her pleasure in his conversation about himself.

And Mildred, his wife, was supremely happy. She glowed with health and good spirits, and gloried in those of her child, to whom she was devoted; she confirmed her popularity with neighbouring houses, and advised her hostess on the order of their invitation. She took vigorous exercise, and was rewarded in appetite and digestion. She paid court to Mrs. Ashton at the dower-house, talking to her of her daughter-in-law with what was accepted as a delicate reticence. But her greatest triumph was in the terms she established between herself and George. He was bored and annoyed, as I have said. He felt that his wife and Skeffington liked to be together, and was very careful to be pleased with the arrangement. On Jack Ashton he looked as on an amiable but stupid dog. Lady Skeffington irritated him; he felt that she was turning herself on to be gracious, and her tone, which was too often the tone of a woman conscious of some imagined eminence, jarred upon him. The shooting wearied him; the conversation wearied him to the last degree. But he had never disliked his cousin's

wife, who indeed had always studied to please
him.   There was something in her absolute
health and abundant vitality which was attractive — as often happens — to an organisation
delicate and somewhat tired.   Her gaiety, so
patently natural and different from Lady Skeffington's, pleased him, whose wife seemed gay
no more.   He was accustomed to her laugh.
And then she was so good-natured, so frank, so
absolutely on the surface.   For these reasons
Mildred was the most acceptable of his guests,
and she was quick to perceive the fact and not
diffident to use it.

On the fourth morning, he excused himself
from shooting and went to his library.   Thither
presently went Mildred, tapped at the door,
and entered with exaggerated softness, demurely
arch.   George laughed and put down his
book.

"I'm most frightfully sorry to disturb you.
I know you'll never forgive me.   But really I
won't keep you a moment.   Minnie Talbot's
written to me to ask if I know of a tutor for
her boy.   He's been super — what is it! — yes,
superannuated from school.   I knew you could
tell me of one."

George wrote down the address of a briefless friend.

"Thank you so much. Now I'll rush away. You must be glad to escape from us frivolous people."

"Oh, please! am I such a bear?"

"No, really, George, I know it must bore you to be always listening to nonsense, and you must want to be with your books. You may not believe me, but I do admire people with brains. I think you give tone to the family — don't laugh, sir: I mean it — poor Jack has n't any brains. And — well, good-bye."

"No; stay and talk."

George looked up at her; he had been very much bored, and you have heard of his temperament.

"You'd hate me for a month if I did. Anything I can do for you before I go? Yes, I see; I'll mix you a brandy and soda."

She mixed a strong one.

"Should n't I make a good barmaid?"

It was indeed the fact, but George merely thought she was a very pleasant and pretty woman. She went out with a kind look over her shoulder. In the passage she met Nelly

and put her finger on her lip. " George is deep
in his books," she said, warningly. She came
on other days to borrow a book, to ask how to
spell a word in a letter, and the like ! And she
was always sympathetic about his brains, and
always mixed him a brandy and soda. And
so something near to an intimacy was established and the days went by. I fear the
course of this narrative is leading away from
ideals.

CHAPTER X

AN UNCONSCIOUS CAMPAIGN

So a fortnight went by and the afternoon arrived on the morrow of which the guests were to leave, and it happened that Mildred Ashton found Lady Skeffington alone in the hall. She sat down on a chair by her friend's side.

" So this is to be our last evening," she said.

" Yes," said Lady Skeffington, with a yawn.

" Are you sorry ? "

" H'm — well. It's a nice place. Are you ? "

" Oh, I should stay if I wanted to. We 're going to the Granleighs in a couple of days. Of course it was convenient, coming; we had nowhere to go and it 's healthy for my boy. Bless him. I like George, too; don't you ? "

" Oh, yes."

" What do you think of his wife ? " Mildred asked, looking at the other. It seemed that neither thought the place inappropriate to the question.

" Frankly? "

" Of course."

" She always was a silly little thing. I don't care about her; I never did. What strikes me is she 's got so dull. I never agreed with the people who said she was clever. Still, she used to talk more than she does. She 's gone off in looks too — not that I could ever see anything in her to rave about. She 's getting so pale and she 's much too thin, I think."

Mildred settled her plump person more comfortably in her chair. " The married state has its cares and responsibilities," she said smiling.

" What a pity they married," said Lucy.

" Why? "

" Why, my dear, if your cousin died without children, your husband would have this place, would n't he! And I 'd come and stay with you."

" Thanks, dearest. But George is younger than Jack — and you must n't talk like that — it 's dreadful to think of benefiting by anybody's death."

Lady Skeffington had acquired a frankness which was not in her training and laughed.

"But he's a much worse life," she said. "He looks delicate — very — and he drinks."

"Oh, my dear!"

"Of course he does. Charlie's pretty bad, but your cousin drinks twice as much as he does. I should say he could n't last."

"How terrible," said Mildred. "But, anyhow, we're out of it now. I hope they'll have children — it will draw them together."

"You ought n't to wish that, you know," Lucy said and regarded her curiously. "If your cousin drinks, his children can't be healthy."

"Ye-es, I see that," said Mildred slowly.

"And, you know, I don't think they will. I mean, they won't live together. They're obviously beginning to hate one another, and then they'll be separated, and you'll be all right. You're safe so far."

I do not think that Mildred's horror of her friend's brutality was wholly affected. In her case, early environment still modified temperament and instinct, and the other's plainness brought a blush to her healthy cheek.

"Don't talk like that, Lucy," she said; "I

don't like it. I'm sure I shall do my best to keep them friends. I don't altogether like her. It was a grief to us — to George's mother and me — when they married, but I shall do my best for her."

" Of course you will, dear angel." She patted Mildred's hand, and Mildred's indignation seemed to be appeased.

" Where are the men? "

" George and Jack are playing billiards."

" And Charlie 's loafing about with our sweet hostess," and Lady Skeffington laughed, but Mildred looked at her with an appearance of sympathy.

" Oh, I don't mind," she answered the look.

" It 's an innocent amusement."

" But don't you think it 's a pity? Of course it does n't matter with us, but in the world people might say — do you know I think I ought to say something."

" Oh, don't bother about me." Lady Skeffington did not care, but then she was bored.

" Well, it 's for her sake. Perhaps if I said a word to George's mother — I should hate doing it, but it might be right."

Lady Skeffington looked at her humorously.

"You sweet, unselfish angel. Well, dear, play your own game — I mean, do what's right. I'm going to look at the billiards."

She went, leaving it uncertain whether it was in her interests or in Nelly's that Mildred Ashton was to say a word.

And Mildred sat in thought. I think it a mistake to credit her with conscious conspiracy. Lady Skeffington's former suggestion had really shocked her; the latter one she pushed aside at once. She was sure she would be doing right in making an effort to keep scandal from Nelly Ashton. A vulgar scheme to bring about a quarrel and a separation did not present itself to her mind. No; it was her duty to stop this flirtation with Skeffington. And meantime it was charitable to show a little kindness to poor George. She welcomed him with her brightest smile as he came from the billiard room.

She announced at dinner that if Nelly would be sweet enough to invite her, she would like to stay two days longer, and go straight to the Granleighs, joining her husband (who had business there) on her way through town. Accordingly, on the next morning the Skeffingtons and Jack Ashton drove away from Rowe, while Mildred at the door held up the crowing boy to wave good-bye to his father. It was a pretty picture; George and Nelly Ashton were somewhat in the background.

In the afternoon Mildred went to the dower-house. She found old Mrs. Ashton reading in the porch, and sat down on a stool by the side of her garden chair.

"It's kind of you to come and see an old woman," said Mrs. Ashton. Nelly's visits had been few of late, and, although Mrs. Ashton did not really desire them to be frequent, when one is old one notices a failure of attention.

"You know I love to come," murmured Mildred and laid her hand with diffident affection on the old lady's arm. Mrs. Ashton caressed the sleek young hand with her long white fingers.

"Dear child," she said. "I'm always glad to see you. My boy was here this morning. He said you and he were good friends. I'm so glad — you're so sensible — and so good."

It was an opportunity Mrs. Jack desired, and she explained her difficult task: how she hated to say anything that seemed to disparage George's wife, but how Lucy Skeffington was

her dearest friend and was suffering very much,
although she hid it under her laughing manner; how of course it was all innocent, but
of course poor Lord Skeffington, well, he
had n't a very good reputation, and how perhaps, if Mrs. Ashton spoke a word to Nelly —
Mrs. Ashton shook her head. "I can't," she
said, "but I will speak to George. I know there
is nothing in it, but young girls are thoughtless.
I can't bear that such things should be needful
in the case of my son's wife, but — but you are
good-natured, dear; yes, it 's very good-natured
of you. Yes. I 'll speak to George, poor
boy."

That was what Mrs. Jack, in the interest of
everybody, wished, and she kissed Mrs. Ashton
on parting with real kindness. As she walked
away she even graciously revised her former
judgment and said to herself that Mrs. Ashton
was really a dear old thing. George went to
see his mother again in the evening, and after
breakfast the next day, while Mrs. Jack strolled
to the hall door to sniff the air, he followed his
wife into the drawing-room.

"I want to say something, Nelly. I daresay
you 'll think me ridiculous, but I must ask you

to forgive that. I don't wish to say anything offensive about anybody. Skeffington is a good chap, and of course I know you 're incapable of anything — anything vulgar. But it is possible to be too good friends with him."

Nelly turned to him angrily. " May I ask if it was your mother or was it Mildred Ashton who suggested this to you? "

" Neither," George said, curtly. " I speak simply from my own observation."

" You didn't say this to Charlie? "

" Certainly not — that would have been to make an exaggerated fuss. But I suppose I can mention such a thing to my wife without doing anything unique."

" Oh, no, it's not unique. It's common enough."

" Exactly."

" Other women do what they like about these things."

He raised his eyebrows. " Yes, there are women who do what they like about these things."

" Do you wish to insult me? "

" I have no such heroic intention."

She walked quickly to the long window which

opened on the terrace and passed out. George sat down wearily in a chair. He swore to himself. Surely, his life was a huge bore. It was all so stupid, so sordid. It was neither serious nor pleasant. Oh, bah, damn! *Vive la bagatelle!* he must look for some pleasure somewhere.

It was then that Mrs. Jack, strolling to the drawing-room door, saw him, and, noticing his depression, determined to enliven him, in the benevolence of her heart. Her methods of coquetry were not subtle; it must be said, however, that she had found them successful. In this instance she went to the library, locked the door, and came back with the key.

"Well, George," she said, and stopped on the threshold of the drawing-room.

He looked up, and as the sun fell full on Mildred in her trim morning dress, in her radiating health and rosy comeliness, she made a very delightful picture to the man who was cross and had a momentary desire for light pleasure.

"Well?" he said, and got up from his chair.

"You're not going to shut yourself up in the library this morning."

"Certainly not, if I can do anything for you."

"I did n't say you could do anything for me; I said you were not going to shut yourself up in the library. And the reason is that I 've locked the door, and I 've got the key."

She walked impudently up to him, shook the key in his face, and put her hands behind her back, looking archly upon him.

"Woman!" he said, with a tolerable effect of melodrama. "How dare you? Give me the key!"

She clasped her hands, holding the key, in prayer before her, and put her head on one side. "You would n't hurt a weak woman!" she said. At this moment Nelly paused at the window and looked in. Mildred saw her, but George's back was turned.

"Well!" said Mildred.

George caught her soft wrists, and gave a light laugh.

"You know, Mildred, if we 're cousins enough for you to lock up the library, we 're cousins enough for me —"

She shot a look into his eyes, and he bent forward and kissed her cheek.

"Oh!" she cried, and broke away from him laughing, and throwing him the key.

She ran after Nelly. George saw his wife walking away, and remembered their conversation. The humour of the silly *tu quoque* amused him, but as he walked to his library he included Mrs. Jack in a general malediction, which was unjust aud ungrateful.

Mildred ran after Nelly, and linked her arm. "My dear child, surely you're not angry at such a silly thing?"

"Certainly not — why should I be?"

"You know, George and I have been close friends for years, and he always was a flirt — in a harmless way."

"Perhaps that's why he sees it in others." She bit her lip the moment she had said it.

Mrs. Jack took her up at once. "What, he hasn't been scolding *you*? Why, then you can turn the tables. But, really, it's all childish, you know — staid married people and that." In rapid self-justification she decided that George must have spoken too seriously to his wife, more seriously than she, the benevolent Mildred, had intended.

After lunch, Mrs. Jack went to say good-bye

to some especial friends, and George shut himself in the library.

Nelly sat in her room and meditated, a hurtful process with her, as always. So her husband, who presumed to find fault with her loyal friendship with Charlie Skeffington, could himself have a vulgar flirtation with such a vulgar thing as Mildred. This was what was beneath his culture and long words and solemn phrases. And she had thought it was to be a new life for her. And — and her reflections were foolish and piteous. She worked herself at last into a small act of folly which only a foolish young woman could have done. Before dinner she went to Mrs. Jack's room with the bracelet her husband had given her three weeks before.

"I want to give you a present," she said. "This thing does n't suit me at all. Will you accept it?"

Mrs. Jack held out a prompt hand, and looked at the bracelet. She divined the cause of the gift, and had a momentary doubt of the wisdom of acceptance. But stones are stones, and these were beautiful and costly. If these foolish people must quarrel, it was not her fault; George was too sensible to blame her.

"Oh, my dear, it's lovely, but you must n't give away your jewels like this."

"I really don't want it. Will you wear it at dinner?"

"Of course I will. It's sweet of you, dear. Thanks so very much." She kissed the giver lightly; there was no use in exaggerating an obligation. Nelly drew back slightly from the kiss, as Mrs. Jack noticed.

At dinner she anticipated the inevitable — and perhaps prevented a possible recall — by holding out her wrist towards her host.

"Look what your prodigal wife has given me."

"I thought it suited her better than me," said Nelly with a quivering lip.

George looked at the bracelet carelessly. "Yes, I think it suits Mildred better than you," he said.

Mrs. Jack ate and talked for the three; George consulted his glass; poor Nelly had no resource. But though Nelly was silent in the drawing-room, and though George went back to the library after ten minutes of their society, Mrs. Jack continued to babble cheerfully, and, having first embraced her sleeping baby, went to bed in perfect good humour. I should say she was triumphant, but that, I am certain, there was no consciousness in her reasoning mind of having made a clever stroke in a sordid game. And while the others lay with set and wakeful faces, she slept the smiling sleep of those who are just to themselves.

CHAPTER XI

"LIFE'S A FARCE"

THE next morning Nelly kept her room, and
George had the privilege of meeting Mildred
tête-à-tête at breakfast.   He was pale and fidgety
and ate nothing; Mrs. Jack talked placidly, and
placidly proceeded through a substantial meal.
Presently George rang for a brandy and soda,
and straightened himself when he had drunk it.

"I wish you'd stay longer," he said.

Mildred looked at him gravely.   "I'm afraid
I can't, George;   and, do you know, I'm not sure
it would be wise if I did.   You won't mind my
saying something?   You know I'm really your
friend."

"I know you are."

"That's right, dear George.   I am, indeed.
Well, I could n't help seeing last night that Nelly
and you had quarrelled about something.   That
distresses me dreadfully."   She broke the shell
of her second egg and regarded it with a sorrow-

ful expression. "I know it hasn't anything to do with me, but somehow I feel I don't make things better. Nelly doesn't like me, I'm afraid. I've tried my best, indeed I have."

"I know you have, Mildred; you've been awfully good."

He held out his hand towards her. She was sitting on his right, and her left hand was encumbered with toast and butter. A sentiment was convenient.

"I hate to see people I care for unhappy in any way," said Mildred, and, her hand being free, she took his in a frank grasp of friendship.

"You know," she continued, "I didn't at all like to accept that bracelet, but I was so afraid of offending her. I couldn't help thinking it had something to do with your having disagreed; forgive me if I'm interfering. I should like to give it back to her if I possibly could."

"Oh, nonsense; it's awfully good of you, but Nelly has lots of toys, and she won't miss that one."

"No; I shall insist on giving it back, and you may give me something instead, if you like," she said gaily. He expressed a polite gratification.

"I think I shall run up to town for a day or two," he said; "what train do you go by?"

"The eleven. Are you really going to town? Then we can go together, and we'll go to a shop and you can buy me some trifle instead of the bracelet. That'll be very jolly and friendly."

George went to his wife's room and announced his intention.

"You won't be bored for a couple of days? I suppose it would n't amuse you to come up too? There's nothing to do in London now. I shall take a room at the club and come back as soon as I've done my business."

"Oh, I shall be all right, thanks. I suppose you are going with Mildred? Well, I hope you'll enjoy yourselves."

"A wise man never expects enjoyment," George said, but added with a quick change to lightness, "in this ass of a world."

"Good-bye," said Nelly evenly, and he left the room.

Mrs. Jack had received a message of apology and farewell from her hostess, but was of a friendliness not to be withstood. She tapped at the bedroom door and entered immediately with the smiling nurse and the noisy baby.

Nelly put her hand to her forehead when she
saw the intruding host. She kissed the baby
perfunctorily, and he was carried out by the
almost visibly indignant nurse. Mrs. Jack remained standing by the bedside. Nelly was
lying in a tumbled heap of fluffy lace stuff, her
beautiful hair brushed back with her hands from
her face, the romance of her beauty pointed by
pallor and heavy eyes. Perhaps it was appreciation of beauty that caused Mildred's bright-
ness as she looked down. Nelly looked up, and
dropped her eyes. She felt oppressed, as
though the affable Mildred were some full-
bodied fate standing over her in triumph, and
she longed for her to go.

"It's been so jolly, dear," said Mildred.

"I was so glad you could come."

"But everything comes to an end."

"Yes," said Nelly.

"One thing, dear — I want to give you back
that bracelet. It was very sweet of you, but I
don't like to keep it. I know George gave it
to you —"

"Did he tell you?"

"Oh no, dear; I guessed, really," she laughed.
"It's all a joke. Here it is, dear."

She put the bracelet on the bed.

"I'm sorry you don't like my present. I thought you did."

"Oh, nonsense, dear, it's not that. I won't take it. Poor dear, you look feverish." She laid her hand on Nelly's forehead, who winced at the touch.

"I'm rather headachy. I think, if you won't think me rude, I'll try to get some sleep."

"That's right, dear, you're not at all well. I'll tell George he must n't stay away more than a day."

Nelly sat up rigidly in bed and broke out.

"Really, Mildred, this is too much. George and I can really manage ourselves without your advice."

Mrs. Jack laughed tolerantly. "You poor child, you must be bad. Why, I only suggested I might tell George you're not well; men can't notice that as well as women. I'm awfully sorry if I annoyed you."

Nelly had seen her mistake at once: she must either make a scene and express vague grievances, as she was too proud to do, or she must admit that she had been rude without provocation.

" I beg your pardon. I'm rather ill, I think; my nerves are rather upset."

Mrs. Jack became a frankly superior being. "Yes, that's it, dear; you must take care of yourself. But do remember I only want to do what is kind. There — good-bye."

Quite coolly she patted Nelly's cheek, and turning away before any possible protest could be made was gone in triumph.

As the door closed Nelly laid her face for a moment on the pillow. Then she left her bed, and walked rapidly up and down the room. She went to a looking-glass and turned from it angrily. She looked out of the window and clenched her hands. She rang the bell and dressed quickly and left the house, and as she walked to the railway-station she had the motion of one who would outstrip thought. There she wired to Lord Skeffington at his club in London: " Come to me at once. I need you." But thought is winged, as we know, and Nelly loitered and wavered as she walked back to the house. A peal of thunder broke as she entered it, but Nelly was no spectator of herself, and missed the gratification which the dramatic effect would have given her husband in a like emergency. The storm sent a riding neighbour in to lunch, who regretted the absence of Mildred Ashton, and so thought was routed, and the time passed until Skeffington should come.

Her visitor was gone, and she sat in her sitting-room with a railway book on her lap. She consulted it and threw it away. She picked it up and consulted it again, and sat in thought. Sometimes her brows puckered, sometimes she smiled, and once she laughed outright, to look immediately straight before her with hopeless eyes. At length Lord Skeffington's arrival was announced, and she told the butler that she would see him where she was. The old man was trained to insensibility, but when he had shut the door behind him, he sighed to himself and then smiled. There is a pleasure in an intrigue even to the attached domestic.

Skeffington's smile was sweet as ever, but the trouble in his eyes was obvious even to Nelly. He sat down awkwardly; the idea crossed his brain that his position was like a doctor's or a family solicitor's.

"Well, dear, what is it? Awfully lucky: I was just leaving town."

"The end's come, Charlie; that's all."

"Tell me."

"I can't go on with it, Charlie. It's no use trying any more. If he cared for me still, even, I might. Do you know yesterday I saw him kiss Mildred Ashton, and to-day he's gone to town with her."

Skeffington's eyes were humorous. "Well, but," he said, "surely there's nothing in that."

"Oh, nothing in one sense, no. It means he can't care for me now, that's all. If he can be attracted by a fat, vulgar woman —"

"It's not a crime to be fat —"

"Don't take that tone. Leave her out altogether. The fact remains that he does n't care for me. If he did, I would — I would stay. My life's one long misery — oh, one long misery" — she gave a little sob — "but I would do my duty if he cared. I hate the life; I hate the place; it's all wrong. I'm surrounded by people who hate me and I hate them, I hate them. But if he cared — Charlie, do you care?"

"Yes, dearest, I care. But listen to me. You exaggerate things. Your husband's not the type of man you've known best. I daresay he's reserved, and that sort of thing. But he does n't ill-use you — does he? — and he lets you do as you like —"

"Oh, stop, stop. As if that were the point!
You know it's not. It's chivalrous of you to
stick up for him —"

A keen sense of humour which could be self-
contempt was Skeffington's, in spite of George
Ashton's verdict on him, and a look dashed
across the eyes he lowered. He knew very
well why he stuck up for Nelly's husband.

"There's no need," she went on; "I don't
say anything against him. But I can't bear
my life, and I don't think I owe him any duty
now. He's quite cold and indifferent to me.
That woman makes my life a curse, and he
doesn't see, or he won't see."

"There I think you're wrong," said Skeffington quietly. "So far as I can see, this Mrs.
Jack Ashton means you nothing but kindness. Possibly she's not too refined and that,
though, upon my word, I don't see that she's
not. If you don't like her, you needn't see
her, I suppose. But it's absurd to blame your
husband."

"You're all on his side."

"I'm on your side, Nelly, whatever you
do or say."

The voice was friendship's, and the girl took

it, as others have taken it before now, for love's.
She looked at him softly.

"Well, Charlie?"

"Well, dearest?"

"You must know why I sent for you;" she
spoke firmly and frankly. Skeffington stooped
over her and kissed her hair. "My dearest,"
he said. And then he walked to the window
and looked out. The trouble in his face gave
way to a faint smile. The way of women!
They imagine, he thought, that any man is
ready at any moment to run away with any one
of them. What utter folly! How on earth
could they live? He was dependent on his
wife; Nelly had nothing. It was insane, impossible. Then the man thought deeply for
a moment. He had loved this woman in a sort
of way, and such love as he had borne her
had by frankness and good comradeship been
turned to friendship. Now he loved her no
more, and she asked him to sacrifice all the
little joys of his life for the pretence. He
knew her well enough to know that she wanted
him to take her away, did not want a secret
intrigue. Yes — but — but — you see his position was intolerably humorous. He was fixed

against taking her away, and he made a poor
figure there, but if he persuaded her, as he
might, that nothing matters, that her husband
could never know — I do not credit Skeffington
with this analysis; he convinced himself for a
moment that there was a return of love. But
while there was no strong barrier in his code
of honour against a secret love with his friend's
wife, there was a barrier of a sort, nor was there
passion for the woman in him to break it down.
But quite unintellectual Irishmen are keen to
feel the humour of themselves. So Skeffington
sat down by her side, and took her hand and
kissed it, while her mouth pouted.

"You see, my dearest," he said, "in this
stupid world of ours we have to face facts."
She drew her hand away and turned in her
chair and looked at him. "Yes, facts. We're
not two children. You know my life, and you
know we could not be happy cut off from everything. Suppose I were to consent — suppose I
were to persuade you to leave your husband
and come abroad with me, what would happen?
I should love you for ever, but could we really
be happy?"

She gasped, and then drew herself together.

"Suppose," she said, "that I am ready to face hardships, to face starvation? Suppose I asked you to do this?"

"Oh, my dear," he said, "it would be to escape from what you don't like, not for my sake. It would be utter folly!"

For once in his life Skeffington had a vision of beauty insulted and yet triumphant, of sex supreme looking down with contempt on sex unworthy. He was right, and poor Nelly Ashton was wrong, very likely, but for a moment she thought she had meant but consuming love, and so she looked at him. But the look passed, and she was merely a sad woman as she said: "That's all, Charlie; good-bye."

"Ah, but —" he could not then but assert himself. "Need we be utterly unhappy because —" and then the door opened, and George Ashton came into the room.

All the way in the train Mildred had spoken with superior kindness of his wife and had urged him not to remain away from her. It was not perhaps the course a supremely wise person, who wished to reconcile them, would have chosen; the best intentioned of us cannot be supremely wise. George felt angrier and angrier with his wife, but he came to think it might be unpleasant wisdom and kindness to return that day. He went to a jeweller's shop with Mildred, who chose a ring of about twice the value of the bracelet. The shopman showed him the price in silence, and he credited Mrs. Jack with ignorance while the man smiled inwardly; but the incident did not increase his cheerfulness. London was used up and dirty and empty. He was cross with it, and finally he took an early afternoon train to the country. He walked from the station, and, seeing the butler in the hall of his house, was told that Lord Skeffington and his wife were in her sitting-room. He went there quickly.

Skeffington rose with something like alacrity. George Ashton did not see if the expression which preceded the friendly smile was embarrassment or relief. " How are you, Ashton?"

" How do you do?" He touched Skeffington's hand and turned to his wife. " You didn't tell me of this pleasure," he said.

" No; I thought of it after you went to town. I wanted to consult Charlie about something, and wired to him."

" It was very good of you to come."

" Not at all, I was glad to be of any use. But
I expect I ought to be trotting; my train goes
at half-past six."

" Have you looked it up?" Nelly asked.

" Yes," he said with something like irritation.
She said good-bye to him with indifference,
and George followed him silently out of the
room. Skeffington may be pardoned by an
epicurean if he cursed the whole affair in his
heart.

" I'll walk with you to the station," said
George.

They went in silence for a few minutes and
then George Ashton, speaking with coolness a
little overdone, — " If it is not too great a
secret, I should like, as an outsider, to know if
my wife wanted to consult you on anything
serious."

Skeffington gave a little sigh of relief, and
leant against a tree.

" Look here, Ashton," he said, " I know you
must think me a most impertinent brute for
coming down like this. What happened was
that Mrs. Ashton wished to consult me about
something that was worrying her. You'd gone

9

to town, and I suppose she did n't wish to bother you. I 'm one of her oldest friends, and she knew I 'd be delighted to advise her if I could. So she wired to me."

"I quite see," said George; "the subject of the advice —"

"Simply it seems there 's been a quarrel between her and Mrs. Jack Ashton —"

"Oh, damnation!"

The two victims of feminine animosity laughed. Both, you see, had a sense of humour; and George Ashton did not believe he had any grievance against Skeffington, and Skeffington was irritated against George's wife. They parted friends.

"Her nerves are over-wrought," said Skeffington. "If I may say so without interfering, I think the truest kindness would be not to take any notice of this business about Mrs. Jack."

And so it was that Nelly Ashton was overwhelmed with kindness.

CHAPTER XII

OLD FRIENDS TO THE RESCUE

ABOUT seven months later George Ashton was walking slowly along Piccadilly westwards in the late afternoon.   He had lunched at his club, and remained there talking aimlessly and drinking with an aim of which he was half-conscious. His pale face was touched with a red that was not of health, and his eyes were slightly sunken. He walked on the north side and gazed at the trees on the other with a sort of vague recollection that once he had enjoyed the sight of Piccadilly in the spring.   He was presently tapped on the shoulder and started.

"Crime or debt or nerves?" said a cheerful voice.   Mr. Francis Wilmot was as straight as ever, ruddy, and a little bronzed.   As the two men shook hands youth was all on the side of the elder.   But George's face brightened as he looked at his friend.

" It was nerves, it might have been debt, and one of these fine days, if the world does n't conduct itself better, it will be crime. You 're still growing younger, Francis; got down to about eighteen. When did you come back — Italy, was n't it ? "

" Yes ; a week ago, my boy. Been down to Wiltshire ; just back. I 'm on my way to Half-Moon Street : your mother sent me the address."

" So was I ; the devil sent me the address — I mean it 's rather a cormorant of a little house. It 's awfully nice of you ; we 'll go together."

" Yes," said Mr Wilmot, " these little houses are expensive. But it 's all right about that kind of thing, I suppose ? "

" All right? My dear Francis, I'm on the verge of ruing, with a g." It was not the confidence of wine ; George Ashton was never reticent about material things. " You see, Rowe bores my wife, — but I must n't put it on to her, — it bores me. We 've taken this house in Half-Moon Street for a year, took it in October, in fact, and of course Rowe costs something to keep going. I 'm thinking of letting it to Jack."

" But I thought there was a tradition — "

" Oh, hang tradition." Mr. Wilmot looked at

him gravely. "One's fathers lived in better
times. Besides, Jack's an Ashton; in fact he
seems to think that entitles him to have it at
about a tenth of the right rent. It's really the
most sensible thing. We're pretty well broke,
and Mildred's father died some months ago and
left her a lot of money. Died in a very respectable, Illustrated London News — wills, you know
— sort of way, 'at his house, the Rookery,' or
whatever it was called, at Highgate." Mr. Wilmot grew graver as the other grew more voluble.
"She lent — I mean it's really the most convenient plan. I think of going to Africa or the
Wild West or some place to — look at it, and my
wife would be infernally bored alone at Rowe.
You see, Francis, we've finished our honeymoon.
That sounds like theatrical pathos, does n't it?
I don't mean anything serious, and you 're a very
old friend."

"Yes, my boy, I'm a very old friend, and I
shall try to act as one."

"Thank you, Francis," said George and then
laughed. "Don't be too old a friend, though.
It would be thrown away."

They walked on in silence to the corner of
Half-Moon Street, when George asked if Mr.

Wilmot liked menageries. "Because with any luck you'll see a very fair one. A few writing chaps of the baser sort, one or two of the shadier order of plutocrat, and perhaps a notoriously evil liver — the only decent element, and a young man whom heaven designed for a lady's maid. Add some dubious actresses and some —"

"Where are your friends?"

"My wife's friends are mine; that's right, isn't it? Mildred Ashton comes pretty often, and my wife will hardly speak to her. I should say she was almost the only real friend we have."

"I must be older than I expected, George, for somehow I don't like the way you talk."

George looked at his friend as he took out his latch-key.

"I assure you I haven't meant a word I said — except that Mildred's a good friend. Good fortune makes me irresponsible."

He fumbled with the key and Mr. Wilmot said nothing. When they entered the drawing-room, there was no menagerie; there was but one person besides Nelly, and it was Lady Tremayne.

George's saturnine querulousness vanished
at once. The visit was unexpected. Sir
Maurice had had a sudden reaction to cheerfulness and health, and had insisted on coming
at once to London and the House of Commons,
and they had arrived but the day before. The
cordiality of the fact was emphasised in Lady
Tremayne's words; temperament and habit
compelled an earnestness of expression which
gave George, now a little sunk in cynicism, a
slight feeling of awkwardness. Nelly, at war
with the world, permitted herself a faint smile
which her husband saw and resented. But
presently she was engrossed by the chatter of
Francis Wilmot, and George talked freely and
with relief to Lady Tremayne. It was to him
like smelling some dear and forgotten perfume;
disappointed passion is not healed in this way,
but a starved brain and sympathy went out to
her, and the old relation was in rapid re-estab-
lishment. When she rose to go, she asked
the Ashtons to dine with her on their first free
day. "But I must see you again before then.
I shall be in all to-morrow afternoon."

"Of course I'll come," said George.

"And you too, I hope? We have arrears of
acquaintance to make up."

"I'm afraid I've promised to be at home — thank you very much," said Nelly, "but you will have a lot to talk over with George."

The awkwardness of the remark struck Lady Tremayne, and the smile of conventional cordiality, which a real intention of friendliness had repressed, appeared on her face.

Mr. Wilmot looked gravely on the proceedings. In common with many men of his age, a relation other than acquaintanceship or maternal friendship between a woman of thirty-six and a man five years her junior, annoyed him, and remembering past gossip he was not sure of the relation in this case. He had reinstated himself as champion of Nelly, and guessing the turn events had taken, was inclined to blame the husband exclusively. These modern young men, he thought, these clever young men, with their ideas and their paradoxes and their views of life and their infernal nonsense, did not know how to manage a girl. When he was young, a beautiful, spirited girl — she had been spirited — like this one would have been happy with him, and then he thought of George Ashton's mother and at once was kindly towards George, and, looking keenly in his face, remem-

bered his father. Poor boy, his path of life was
tangled before his birth. He shook hands
affectionately with him as he left. " You young
men hate sentiment," he said, " but if you want
a friend, my boy, remember I've known you all
your life."

" A fearful retrospect, Francis; pity chronol-
ogy makes the moral too late. No, don't think
I'm ungrateful — I daresay I shall be trouble-
some to you yet." A slight artificiality of words,
an accident in this case, is an infallible proof of
insincerity to down-right people; Mr. Wilmot's
irritation returned.

As they sat, the next afternoon, in a corner
of the twisted drawing-room in Lowndes Street,
Lady Tremayne looked anxiously at George
Ashton, the while he discussed the import of a
lonely house in Ireland and Sir Maurice's ague.
He kept himself resolutely from his affairs, conscious of course that the omission was signifi-
cant, but unable to talk of them to this old
friend without saying more than he designed.
He was in a different mood from that which had
caused his indiscretion to Mr. Wilmot the day
before, and, moreover, he approached Clara Tremayne with a deeper consciousness. But Lady

Tremayne wanted to hear, and ultimately of course she was told. She had not, however, nor would she have used, that malicious tact by which such confidences are induced to the confider's self-execration. It was a straightforward asking and giving of confidence.

One need not go about to discuss if the confidence were in any way excusable; at least George Ashton made it in the manner of a gentleman, blaming himself much and his wife not at all. He had been a fool, he said, who had made a great blunder, and he had not wisdom or temper to retrieve it. His wife's idea of life was not his, and he despaired of her changing it. He disliked her friends, and his dislike, whether creditable or not, made no impression on her, and his friends had not the luck to be acceptable. But of course she was right to stick to her friends, and right not to play the hypocrite with his. Only, only it was not convenient. And somehow, somehow they did not amuse one another. It may be conjectured that a social philosopher hearing these grievances would have taken them for symbols of something deeper, which, in some base, analytical manner, he would have pretended to discover.

It is certain that Mr. Wilmot would have been so far at one with the philosopher as to brush aside the grievances as unessential and absurd. Lady Tremayne took them seriously as covering the ground ; she deplored and she suggested.

And as she deplored and suggested, the tale of them ended, for the assumption, which she could not but have made, that the woman was wholly in the wrong, clashed against the man's generosity. And she not over resisting, he turned the conversation to themselves. What pleasant times had been ! " Yes, dear George, they were very pleasant." What a muddle the world was ! " Yes, that is it — just a muddle." The lady spoke faintly. A play of sighs, let us call it a comedy. She had not a great deal of humour, but George Ashton had enough for a gibe or two at the world, at fate, and at himself — drawing this superfluous distinction —whereat the lady looked wistful and troubled, and he, seeing the look, pressed her hand and spoke seriously. " Dear friend, it is good of you to care what happens to such a worthless creature ; you were always my best friend."

Lady Tremayne had been very lonely for

many months, brooding, sentimentalising it may be called. She was wearied with constant attendance on her husband, she was weak and had thought too much o' nights. Lady Tremayne began to cry, and George Ashton, as was inevitable, began to comfort her. He was genuinely distressed, and her tears called up in him a tenderness of tone which perhaps he had learned from long intercourse with his mother. What wonder if Clara Tremayne, hysterical for a moment and full of sympathy and regrets, cheated herself? She drooped towards him. It was all innocent in her mind; she had longed for sympathy, as she called it still, and this man had been in her thoughts for long, and they had been the best friends in the world, and he had made shipwreck of his life, she thought.

And so, when George Ashton left the house of his comforter, he had added to the interests of his life a sentimental dalliance with a woman for whom he did not really care. I could tell you with exactitude what view of all this would have been held by Mr. Wilmot. But as folly goes in the world, I think George Ashton's contempt of himself was adequate. He went again to Lowndes Street two days later, all the same,

for response is necessary, and three days after
that he went again, and people who left him
there in possession made their amusing comments, and the world is small.   It came to be
the duty of Mrs. Jack Ashton to remind Nelly
that the best of husbands sometimes need care
in the management of them, and that George
and Lady Tremayne had been talked about
aforetime.   Nelly of course said nothing to
him, but the suggestion, as may happen to the
most good-natured of them, was unhappy in its
issues.

CHAPTER XIII

THE END OF A LECTURE

MR. WILMOT, having talked to Nelly and observed her husband two or three times, and having brought a practical intelligence to bear upon the situation, had taken a resolution. He asked George to dine with him alone at his house, and as they smoked after dinner announced an intention of speaking seriously. George waited despondently, with some of that instinctive nervousness that comes inevitably upon us when those who have known us all our lives take us to task, and we feel something of our childhood's incapacity to answer.

"You see," said Mr. Wilmot, "I knew your father very well, and your mother's my oldest and my best friend. You and I have always been on good terms. — I 've not the slightest right to interfere in your affairs, and you can stop me the moment you think me impertinent. But I 'm a very old friend, and have seen something of life, and sometimes plain speaking is a good thing."

George by this had nerved himself; it was after dinner, and he looked at the old man with a smile.

"That's your experience, is it? But be as plain as you like."

"It's about your wife and you."

"She's always interesting, but could n't you leave me out?"

The tone grated on Mr. Wilmot. "You two are making a mess of things simply for want of understanding one another."

"It sounds like 'he died from ceasing to live,' does n't it?"

"She's a sweet girl, my boy, and you 're not a bad fellow either if it was n't for your modern ideas about things."

"I assure you I have n't a single idea that's newer than Aristippus and Solomon — at least he did n't write Ecclesiastes, did he? You know I always regret those questions of authorship —"

"Say frankly if you wish me to stop."

George paused for a moment. "No, Francis, I beg your pardon; go on."

"I think you 've both got fads about things, but I tell you honestly, I think you are most to blame. A man of thirty who marries a young girl should be able to master her and make her happy just by being her master. Now, you leave her alone, and then you criticise her. A girl ought n't to be criticised; she ought simply to be told what 's best."

"Mohammedan! I don't much like defending myself on such a matter, but I 'll say this much: I thought I was acting for the best in giving her rational liberty."

"Rational liberty be damned!"

"It seems as if it would, certainly. As for criticising her, if she fills the house with a lot of tag-rag, pretentious outsiders — "

"You used to have friends of your own. Why did n't you surround her with them ?"

"Why? I tried — a little. Somehow one's women friends don't swarm round one's wife. My men friends clashed a bit with hers."

"You ought to be independent of friends."

"Oh, of course. But when we had discussed the ideas we had in common — " he broke off with a slight shrug.

"Ideas in common! Upon my soul, George,

you young men appal me! Ideas in common!"

Mr. Wilmot was perplexed. At length he said: "I tell you what it is, George; you ought to have a profession — work. Work."

George laughed naturally. "You 're a little hard up for a remedy, Francis. What useful career does your experience suggest?"

"It 's no use rounding on me, my boy. I never had a minute to spare, though I 've done no work at all. I never had time for morbid notions. Ideas in common!"

"I give that up. I only spoke in the jargon one knows. You know what I meant — we don't seem to appeal — oh, never mind. I 'll take another brandy, if I may."

If Mr. Wilmot had been of his guest's own age, he might have been able to comment without offence on one of his guest's habits, from the point of view of another sufferer. As it was, he could only think in silence that trouble seemed likely to drive this boy in the way of his father. The thought banished all banter from his tone.

"Perhaps I 've said too much, my boy; this is the upshot of it all. I want you to remember your wife 's very young, and that with her plain

speaking and open affection are worth all the
fine ideas and clever criticisms in the world. Be
there more, encourage her to see less dubious
people, even if they 're not so wonderful. Your
cousin Jack's wife for instance — "

" Nelly hates her."

" Ah, yes, she said something like that.
Women have their fads — they don't mean anything. She is n't in good health, you know. But
brace one another up. Pull yourself together,
my boy. Do some work, writing or something
of that sort. Better still, take your wife for a
voyage. Look here, if you 'll let an old friend
do it, I 'll find a yacht and we 'll go together."

" I could n't let you do that, Francis. But I 'll
try to get Nelly to come to Scotland for a week.
You know Bob Adair? He 's one of my oldest
chums, though I 've not seen him of late; he
won't leave Scotland; he and his wife — they 've
not finished their honeymoon, you know. I 'll
ask him to take us in and I 'll remember what
you 've said."

And shortly afterwards he went away and
walked straight to his house. Of course he
thought that Francis Wilmot did not understand
things, was narrow and antiquated. But he was

not blind nor locked in a priggery, this poor husband, and he felt that something in Mr. Wilmot's tone, something in his frank laughter and perplexity, was right and on the side of the nature of things.

His wife was reading in the drawing-room, and he sat down by her side.

"Nelly, I want to say something to you."

She put her finger in the book to keep the place and looked up with intentional indifference.   "Yes?"

He wavered and pulled himself together.

"I know I'm not satisfactory, Nelly; I know you have reason not to be content. I say nothing on the other side. But can't we try to be better friends? If you can't care for me much in one way, can't we still get on together without — without this coldness?"

A while ago, she would have turned to him forthwith. But the time was gone and she met him with this question.

"May I ask if anybody suggested this to you, George?   Did Lady Tremayne?"

He walked across the room, and spoke abruptly from before the fireplace.

"No.   I wish to know why you ask."

"Merely that she seems a great friend of yours."

"She is a great friend of mine. She did not suggest this; there was no possibility that she should. I only — but it's hopeless. Sorry I interrupted your reading."

As he left the room, she looked after him with doubt and trouble. Then she gave an empty little laugh, and turned to her book, to throw it away presently and go to her room.

He asked her the next day if she would come with him to Scotland to stay a week with his great friends, the Adairs, and she said she could not leave her engagements.

"Do you mind if I go for a week? I'm rather seedy."

"A week? Oh, no."

CHAPTER XIV

IN FRESHER AIR

POUF! It is pleasant, as the train goes north, to let down the window for a healthy smack from the blithe fresh air. Pouf! It rushes through the railway carriage and drives out of t' other window London and dust and grime and blurred ideals, and perverse developments, and all unwholesome communications. George Ashton was leaving behind him for a space the troubles of his or others' making, his wavering restless sorrow, his tedious distractions, his weary comedy of consolation. A painted, hollow life he felt it to be, unworthy, almost vile. He knew it was a man's business to master it or break through it, and he knew he was failing miserably, But — pouf! — here was a moment for fresh air. He was on his way to unthinking friendship, to harmless, irresponsible fun, to simple kindness. All of the boy that was left in George Ashton was agog to be there.

Meanwhile his hosts were sitting over a late breakfast, and the kind gods saw no happier little party in these isles than Bob Adair, and Fanny his wife, Madeleine his sister, and Tommy Tucker his wife's cousin. Bob Adair's father had married a Frenchwoman, and Bob, at least, was more French than English. His father had cared for his wife's country better than for his own, and Bob and his sister had lived most of their lives in France, the former being educated by an English tutor until he was old enough for Oxford. Two years before this narrative, he had married the sister of an Oxford chum, and, his father dying shortly afterwards, had tried the experiment of living in the house which descended to him in Dumfriesshire, to pleasure his wife's national predilections, and to favour secluded love. The experiment was a great success, and with the exception of a short visit to Paris and to London they had remained cooing in Dumfriesshire — Bob was a barrister by profession — ever since. They were an unending delight to one another. Fanny was a Scotchwoman of a type one knows,

compact of life and kindliness, good breeding
and common sense. Bob was an Anglicised
Frenchman, a good sportsman, and a perfect
host, with a thousand pretty homages for his
wife, a thousand harmless, irrepressible follies.
He laughed at and worshipped her prejudices
and her occasional stateliness; she loved and
marvelled at his gaiety and quickness and per-
petual amusement. They were seldom without
a guest or two to behold their happiness — Bob
especially craving for the world to salute and
sympathise — and never a guest but envied and
granted it was deserved.

Everybody knew Tommy Tucker, whose real
Christian name was Alexander. His age was
twenty-five years, and sometimes he seemed to
be thirteen, and sometimes about three hundred.
He talked incessantly, sometimes with penetra-
tion and with wit, more often sheer inanity.
His profession was having been private secretary
to an eminent actor, and intending to go some
day to South Africa. Most people thought him
an amiable idiot, a few that he was a genius in
disguise, and nobody took his words or his
actions seriously. Nobody but liked him; the
first instinct of everybody would have been to

laugh at any conceivable misfortune that could have happened to him. The idea of Tommy in a railway accident, or of Tommy as the victim of an unhappy love would have seemed obviously ludicrous. And if Tommy had his share of human woes, he was never known to mention them or only from a humorous point of view. Yet he was called upon very often to sympathise with other peoples' debts and lamentable emotions. In appearance he was a stout young man, beautifully dressed, and with very neat hair. He was thought to be a lover of the pavement, but now he stayed away from the London season in content, for the sake of his board and lodging, he told his entertainers, who said he was rather a nice thing to have about the house. This was the view of the world concerning Tommy Tucker, whom it seemed to satisfy.

There was never a photograph of her taken in the least like Madeleine Adair. Looks shot across her face like ideas in a quick brain. In repose it was very grave for her age, which was twenty-two, but with a gravity individual and various. It was seldom in repose, however, but lighted for this or that chance remark from this

or that person. She had lived all her life with
people more than commonly amiable, and with
them exclusively, and had therefore neither
diffidence nor distance in her manner. Her
gaiety was as constant and as ready as her
brother's, but she had not his universal lightness.
Certain subjects made her grave — subjects,
partly, that are absurdly thought to have reached
our women yesterday for the first time — and on
them she could speak to her brother or his wife
with eagerness, and with something of French
logic and detachment of mind. Her mother,
between whom and her there had been love
without reserve, had died when she was seven-
teen, and her father had made her his constant
companion. For the three years between then
and his death she read and talked constantly
with him on lines that were commoner for
women in Elizabeth's time than in the generations nearer our own, if our own, as some think,
has really reverted to them. On his wife's death,
her father's love of the ways of men had deserted
him, and although he did not shut himself from
French society, he fell back more and more
on books and abstractions. He was grown too
French to leave France permanently, but what

had been an innocent worldliness was succeeded
by its antithesis, which his education made possible. Madeleine was accomplished and she had
been taught how to think. She was a beautiful
girl in ordinary eyes and for eyes that could
see had a beauty that, sympathetic or not to
them, was there to remember for ever, an ideal.
Black hair parted over a forehead where brains,
for once, seemed to be at peace with beauty, a
pale fine face, its chin distinct and firm, its
mouth delicately carved, its nose a little long
and perfectly straight, large eyes, dark brown
and heavy-lidded, made for archness, you would
have said, in a face less fine, in her prone to a
friendly irony — these bald facts may help to fix
what the outline of her history has suggested.
Her cheeks were rounded girlishly; she would
have been thought tall before our age of giant-
esses, and her figure was slight and erect. Mrs.
Adair, a very few years older than she, thought
her a dear scatterbrain and regarded her with
maternal protection. To Bob she was a sort of
better self.

"Mr. Ashton's coming by the morning train,
Maddo," said Mrs. Adair, "instead of to-night;
so we shall have him to dinner."

"I wonder how he's altered," said Madeleine. The habit of French had merely given a distinctness to her English, balancing prettily the Scotch distinctness of Mrs. Adair. "It is eight or nine years since I saw him at Oxford."

"Altered a good deal," said Bob. "He was always moody, you know, and had alarming fits of seriousness, and the disease seems to have become chronic. When I saw him in town last he looked responsible for all our sins. Since his marriage you know."

"Yes, it does make a chap look rather an ass," said Tommy.

"Nice Tommy!"

"Oh, you're different; you only play at it."

"We'll marry you to somebody if you don't take care, little boy."

"At Trinity Church I met my doom," chanted Tom who could fit you a music hall refrain to sentiment or situation, and Madeleine laughed and smiled at him. He went on talking at once. "Let me see; Ashton, where does he come in? I've met him, but what is he? I hope he does something; I hate a fellow who wastes his life, every man ought to have a profession, barrister or secretary or something. Got a place somewhere, has n't he?"

"Yes, Rowe," said Bob; "a charming old house, I stayed there often when I was at Oxford. A mother too, dear sweet old lady."

"Oh, of course if he's a squire and a good son, I daresay he fills a proper place in the community. Chap can't do everything."

"Yes, and now he has a beautiful wife."

"I know; I met her ages ago when I was a boy," said Tommy in melancholy cadence. "And I suppose they're happy all day long. I like to see it in the young."

Bob Adair and his wife joined eyes for a moment.

"She won't come," said Mrs. Adair; "I was so sorry. She's really very lovely, Maddo."

"About meeting him," said Bob. "I suppose we must go to those excellent people in the afternoon, Fan?"

"If Mr. Ashton won't think it rude; it's a long engagement."

"All right; Tommy can meet him."

"No, I'll go," said Madeleine, "you can tell the Grays I am ill, and it will be more friendly to Mr. Ashton. He would think the whole affair was a burlesque if he was met by Tommy. I'll take the dog-cart."

"Is that all right, Fan?" asked Bob with immense anxiety. "Do the conventions permit it? Are you sure we sha'n't be sent to prison? Will it shock anybody? The station master; I can't allow that excellent man to be driven into downward courses by bad example."

"I think she can go," said Mrs. Adair, with a simple air of deciding a matter of real importance, at which Bob laughed.

"Besides, Tommy can go too."

"It's risking my life—"

"Oh, Tommy frightens the horse—"

And ultimately Tommy did not go. Bob spoke to his sister with an unusually serious air later that morning. "You know, Mad," he said, "George Ashton's a very great friend of mine. He was my best chum at Oxford and did me more than one good service. His mother, too, was very kind to me; you know I was pretty well alone in England then. We've kept up the intimacy, though we've not seen each other much."

"Yes, dear, I know—"

"Well, but there's a special reason for saying it. There's no harm in telling you that he's in great trouble. Two or three people have told me; his cousin's wife, for instance, a very English but very good sort of woman, hinted pretty plainly that he and his wife — you understand. He shows it too, very plainly, in his way of looking and talking. I want him to feel down here that he's really among friends, people who care for him — something more than ordinary hospitality. Fanny's known him more or less for years and likes him, and I'm sure you'll like him too. You see what I mean? That's why I let you go to the station — "

" Let me go? Baby brother ! "

" Mad Maddo — so that he might get the right impresssion at first. I really feel about this. In fact, I rather wish Tommy wasn't here ; it would make things easier in a way."

" Don't send poor Tommy away, dear. But you really are a nice old boy. Dear Bobby ! "

" That's all right, then. One has such a jolly time oneself, that in the case of a real friend — you see, Maddo."

So spoke, in the simple warmth of his heart, Bob Adair, most affectionate of brothers.

CHAPTER XV

FOLLY

So when George Ashton, the only passenger, got out of the carriage at the little station, he was aware of a slight and tall young figure in a close-fitting dress, of an outstretched hand, of a beautiful face smiling welcome upon him.

"You don't know me, Mr. Ashton? I'm Bob's sister."

"Of course I do;" and indeed he remembered very well the girl of thirteen who came with her beautiful, gracious mother and Bob Adair to his rooms at Oxford, — a thoughtful little girl, grave but not shy, with long black hair and serious heavy-lidded eyes. He looked curiously at the development, the perfectly finished features, the character in the chin and the suggestion of irony in the eyes, and as he looked there came on him, as on all men who have any grace about them, when first they see a finely beautiful

girl, a feeling that — consciously or not — is
reverence. She talked gaily of his journey and
Bob's messages as they walked to the dog-cart,
and she started the horse at a sharp trot, sitting
very upright as she drove.

"Is the world still made of cream cheese, as
you told me at Oxford, and are all the proverbs
still to be taken upside-down ?"

"The world 's made of sanded sugar, and the
proverbs are painfully true."

"Oh, dear! but this is out of the world.
You'll find us all lunatics. I hope there 's a
cap and bells in your portmanteau. If there
isn't, Bob has several to spare, and Tommy
Tucker a hundred at least."

"Is he here? I thought he was going to South
Africa."

"If you tell him that, he 'll be grateful to you
forever. No ; he really won't be allowed to go,
he 's such a dear, sympathetic idiot. I believe we
have a great friend in common, Mr. Ashton, —
Lady Tremayne."

The announcement was not the most delightful
in the world to George Ashton. Talking of nothing to this bright girl, with the fresh wind blowing
in his face, and the pretty country and the un-

familiar stone walls about him, he had forgotten
all his perplexities. Of late his relations to
Lady Tremayne had taken a turn he knew to be
insincere. His friendship for her had been real
and continued, but of late a suggestion of might-
have-beens, and a manner thereunto conforming,
into which he had fallen unwittingly, jarred upon
his honesty. His nerves responded to the recollection; he even had for a moment an absurd
idea that this girl might have heard something
of the intimacy. As a matter of fact, Madeleine
Adair had seen little of Lady Tremayne; with
a simple assurance of response, she always
deemed anybody who pleased her much a great
friend. She had suddenly remembered having
seen a photograph of George Ashton at the
Tremayne's, and that was all.

"Yes, I know her very well. Sir Maurice is
an old friend of my mother's; I used to see them
often at one time."

"The Bruce-Chattertons were some of the
very few English people my father kept up with.
She stayed with us in Paris once, before her
marriage, and my father and I stayed with
them in Ireland three years ago. I heard from
her the other day; in fact I may go to stay

with her in town. Don't you think she's very beautiful?"

The question was as absolutely honest as may be, but George Ashton, remembering Lady Tremayne as he had seen her last, beautiful, certainly, and with a beauty more than that of feature, — our words for these things are too few, — but tired and weary, and looking at length her years, and seeing now this girl in the opening of her powers and her loveliness undimmed, could not choose but compare them. He might have thought (but such thoughts hardly come to us in conversation) that the pathos of her young perfection was something keener than that of Lady Tremayne's life unrealised.

He made the natural answer, and they talked superficially of people and places until they reached the house. But Ashton was refreshed as he had not been for many a day; the girl's musical voice, her distinct intonation, her little friendly, familiar phrases, the kind, frank glances he met now and again, the whole effect of unthinking but never silly innocence and joy, delighted this weary dweller in the dark in a degree few men deserve; the man in him was attracted, and the boy in him was grateful.

Glenburn was a Georgian stone house, of those which are less beautiful than even many a modern house, and yet are infinitely more pleasing to some foolish folk among us, because of the suggestion of a time they love better than their own; you feel (say these) that tragedies not wholly inartistic may have passed behind the windows. Its present use pictorially was, however, to serve as a background to Tommy Tucker, who took the air with slow and careful tread before the hall door. He received Ashton with rather a grave politeness, and at once began to chaff Madeleine on her driving, more freely, George thought, than mirth demanded. Here was a discomposing element at once, a young man who had quite the air of one section of his wife's friends.

But at dinner a surlier man than he would have been forced into amiability. Bob Adair and his sister talked incessant folly, while Mrs. Adair beamed upon them and started fresh trains of it with her common-sense. Tommy was graver than his wont, but presently thawed under Madeleine's mock appeals and made his conversational grimaces. George Ashton laughed, and by-and-bye responded, and, as he did so, Tommy Tucker's politeness relaxed into more friendly rudeness. The talk of this dinner was not the crackling thorns of the Skeffingtons and Ashtons at Rowe. It was intimate, irresponsible, sometimes witty, and therefore shall be left to your imagination. It was wine to George Ashton, but like wine to a convalescent, could be taken only with strangeness and diffidence at first. The bitterness of his life, the sense of hostility he had felt, made it difficult to him to assimilate at once this wine of perfect friendliness and gaiety. But gradually his former mood fell away, and he talked without thinking and with appreciation in his eyes. And so talking, he neglected his actual wine upon the table.

There was music after dinner. Mrs. Adair sang a song or two of her country; Madeleine, whose singing voice was low and sweet and lingering, some simple French songs of the provinces; Tommy Tucker disported his portly frame in a *pas seul*. When George Ashton went to bed he told himself that a weight of years was eased for a while from his shoulders, and alas! did not remember that little more than a year ago he had been the happiest man in the world. No wonder the gods grow tired of blessing.

So the days went by at Glenburn. The fresh
air and the simple life and the unbroken friendliness and fun had a natural effect on George
Ashton. And he was still a young man and the
time was spring. It happened that on three or
four occasions he took long walks with Madeleine Adair, that he sat and talked with her alone,
that he heard her sing when there was none by
to disturb the magic. Bob and his wife had
social duties Madeleine did not choose to share;
Tommy Tucker went away on a three days'
visit to friends in the same county. The world
revolves upon its axis. Here was a man who
had had a romance of the heart and the head,
and the heart had not survived the head's be-
trayal. He had capacity for romance and
worship beyond the common, easy to disturb,
but firm when no disturbance was possible. He
was intensely appreciative of beauty when grace
and manner were its complement. And he was
man enough to feel down in his bones a feeling
which his wife had partly roused, and afterwards
in the chances of life checked pitiably, a tenderness for pure and wholesome youth; and in him
passion which the chances of life had ill-used
was not destroyed. Here was a girl in the first

flower of her womanhood, almost perfectly en-
dowed, and almost perfectly nurtured; fine and
wholesome, kind and delicate and frank.

Here, on the other hand, was a girl of strong
feelings, of grasping brain, quick to perceive
qualities, eager and grateful for response. And
here was a man cultivated beyond question,
and thoughtful, absolutely delicate in expression,
naturally sympathetic, and keen to understand.
And they were alone with a pair of cooing doves
in Scotland.

But George Ashton was married and an
honourable man, and Madeleine Adair was
pure-minded as a poor civilised creature may
be, and conceived no possibility of what she
knew as sin.

They drifted inevitably into intimacy, he telling her of some of his ambitions, which were
broken, vaguely of his troubles, as of part of
his faults; she talking of her life in France, of
her mother, how perfect she was, and of her
companionship with her father.

Tommy Tucker returned rollicking, but after
a day was grave. His manner to Madeleine
changed; the chaff was modified into nothing,
the fits of mock sulkiness disappeared. He

become seriously and evenly cordial; a sort of consideration came into his friendship. He quietly attached himself to her, and followed her in a manner she could not dispute, while she more than once broke out against him, and raked him with criticism. He looked at her very keenly once when this had happened, and she faltered: —

"Dear Tommy, I beg your pardon; indeed I do," and came and shook his hand, and thereafter turned on him no more. On the third day of his return he found Mrs. Adair alone.

"Ashton and Maddo get on well together," he said.

Mrs. Adair looked troubled. "They do," she answered.

"When does he go?"

"To-morrow."

"Will you press him to stay?"

"Why, Tommy? You don't mean —"

"I do mean. Fan, you know I'm not a mean beast. You know what Maddo is to me, and that it's all no use, no use at all." Tommy Tucker took a turn about the room. "I'm not thinking of myself. I'd better go away too, so far as that's concerned. Ashton's a good chap, I 'm sure. But you see how he attracts Maddo; he 's very clever and that, and there 's nobody else. . . . I dare say I 'm a vulgar brute — but it might mean unhappiness to her. Let him go."

"I shall not ask him to stay. Oh, Tommy, you poor boy!"

"Oh, rot about me. That 's of no consequence."

That night was fine, and after dinner Madeleine put on her cloak and invited George to stroll with her, without subterfuge, before the others. They walked up and down the short avenue, talking of abstract things, and by-and-bye sat down on a seat near the house, in silence for a while. Then George made a little gesture of despair.

" If one could stay for ever — "

She did not answer for a minute, and then said softly: "Everything ends. You must go — may I say it? — you must go back to your wife."

"It 's leaving the only heaven I 've known. Forgive me: I 'm a blackguard to talk like that — no, only a fool."

" You must go back to your wife," whispered

Madeleine, faintly. Then she gave a little sob, and turned her head away.

Ashton did not try to comfort her. He sat in silence, hating himself, not even pitying himself, but seeing, or thinking he saw, very clearly, that here might have been the one chance of his life. And Madeleine kept back her tears, had after a minute no need to strive. She faced herself bravely; she pitied him, knowing what all women know; there were things to her impossible. And so for a while these luckless two plighted their trothless troth in silence under the inconstant moon.

The next morning Ashton went away, and Tommy Tucker shook him heartily by the hand, and Bob Adair hugged his sister that afternoon, and went quickly away to curse himself by all his gods.

CHAPTER XVI

MR. MORRISON'S WRONGS

A FEW mornings later Jack Ashton and his wife talked, without the difficulty less healthy people experience, over their breakfast. Mrs. Jack looked particularly well and handsome; the mourning she wore for her respectably deceased father was an advantage to an abundant figure.

"About Rowe," said Jack, "I don't suppose George'll take what we offer. You know he could get three times as much with any luck. We can't expect him to."

"He'll have to," Mildred said. "I've made up my mind about it. It's no use wasting money. I'll manage it all right."

"By Jove, you are clever, Milly. Mean to put the screw on with that thousand you lent him?"

"Not that entirely. You see the way he's going on, he'll have to let it all in a hurry, he

won't do anything till the last moment: he's
not clever about business like you, old pet.
Very well, then we shall stick to our proposal,
and with a little firmness he'll give in. I can
manage him all right. Besides, you know how
they quarrel. They'll have a break up, a separation or something, suddenly one day, and
then it will be quite simple. Of course it's
dreadful to have to think of such things, but
one can't help seeing them."

"It's an awful pity they don't pull together
better. Have some chicken?"

"It's terribly sad — yes, please — it has worried me dreadfully — more of the rice, please;
thanks. One thing, I've really done my best to
make things better."

"Yes, you've been tremendously good-natured, going there so often. I do think Nelly's
awfully ungrateful."

"Well, I've done my best," said Mildred,
complacently. "We must go to Rowe;" she
went on. "You see, dear, it's pretty certain
you'll have it in time, and we may as well have
the advantage of it now. This rent won't make
much difference, and then, supposing they separated, probably old Mrs. Ashton would go to

live with him, and he would n't care to live there. So then we could take on the dower-house and let it again to somebody we liked, — make some improvements or something, and get back the rent on the big house. I 've sketched it all out."

" By Jove, you are a splendid manager."

Mildred's rosy cheeks dimpled with a superior smile of conscious merit.

" But look here," said her husband, " if they separated, George might go to Rowe and live cheap."

" That 's impossible," she said quickly. " He 'd have to make his wife an allowance. He 's been spending his capital; he told me, when he borrowed that money, he 'd lost thousands — betting and cards and things. And they live far beyond their means. I call it dishonest, quite. So we 're quite certain of Rowe, anyhow, whether they separate or not, and I won't give a penny more than I said; we might even get it for less. We 'll get it on a long lease, and then we must be all right. I *think* they 'll separate; of course I shall do all I can to prevent it, but I 'm afraid they will, and if they don't, and if — if anything happened, we could still keep Rowe; he 's sure to spend all the money, — and if anything happened, we could buy it — the entail could be broken then — and of course we should get it cheap."

"And his father-in-law won't leave him anything," Jack said, with a lively sense of heaven's mercies. That was another merit in his wife.

"Poor dear papa," said Mildred, with very decorous solemnity.

"By the way," Jack went on, "I want to bring a man in to lunch to-day if you don't mind — get off early Saturday, you know. City chap. He's an immensely rich beggar, — Morrison's his name, — and I want him to let me into a mining company he's floating — very good thing indeed. I'll tell you about that later. Morrison isn't a bad kind of man," Jack spoke with easy tolerance, "but he's an outsider, you know, and just the sort of man to value a little attention. So you'll be very nice and that sort of thing to him, won't you?"

"Of course I will, old boy. If he's nice and a friend of yours, of course I'll be as charming as I can to him, and I'll order a splendid lunch."

Shortly afterwards Jack, having kissed his wife affectionately, went his way to the City. Mildred lingered over jam and fruit, reading the paper.

Then she consulted for half an hour with her cook, who appreciated appreciation, and went to the nursery, where her boy, to whom she was a fond and wise mother, welcomed her with delight, and the nurse, to whom she was a considerate mistress, with a bright smile. It was an admirable home.

In due course Mr. Morrison arrived with Jack, and found a hostess vastly to his liking. She listened to the tale of his possessions with enthusiasm; she laughed merrily at his jokes; she smiled upon him archly. They must make up a party to go to the play ; he must stay with them in the country. Of course she had no intention of being mixed up socially with Mr. Morrison, who was really — poor man, he could n't help not being quite, quite — but (thought she) it is a duty of hospitality to make people happy. As he held the match to her cigarette after lunch, she favoured him with an upward sweep of her eyelids. Mr. Morrison thought he was flirting with a woman in Society, (the S was very capital in his mind) and plumed himself. The lunch was substantial, as he liked it, but elaborate and ornate; the wine he knew to be good by its brands. Mr. Morrison went away enraptured, and Jack Ashton, having seen him out of the house, went back to his wife with a laughing encomium on her social talents, and she smiled in demure triumph.

Two days later Mr. Morrison called in the afternoon and found Mrs. Jack alone, and was welcomed with gay cordiality. "How nice of you to come so soon!" He announced that he had made Jack a director of the mine, and she clapped her plump hands with girlish glee.

"How splendid, and how very, very kind of you!"

Mr. Morrison explained that it might be in his power to do other services for Jack.

"Dear Mr. Morrison, it is so very sweet of you. I can't tell you how grateful I am. Jack works very hard, poor boy, but you know he's not — not so clever as you," her eyes brightened with appreciation, "and it's everything to him to have some wiser friend to tell him what to do. We can't be too grateful to you."

"Then I hope we shall be friends," he said with unctuous gallantry.

"Of *course* we shall — true friends;" she held out her hand and when Mr. Morrison kept it in his did not withdraw it. Business is business,

you see, and folly is folly; it was silly to mind
such a little thing, and really the man deserved
some kindness.   Mr. Morrison leaned over her
hand with such grace as he had and kissed it.
She laughed, and as she drew it away put a little
pressure into her fingers.

"Now, Mr. Morrison, we must be sensible,"
she said, and the man did not feel repulsed or
offended.   He remembered another Mrs. Ashton whose hand he had not kissed, and her offence grew greater.   He mentioned her name
to Mildred.

"Oh, do you know her?" Mildred sighed.
"Poor little thing," she added.

"I used to see a lot of her before she married.   Her father — I knew him very well."
He spoke bitterly, and Mildred was alert.

"I am afraid I don't like Major Canover,"
she said.   "I don't know anything about these
things, but Jack says he's not — not quite honourable in business matters."

"I should rather think he was n't," said Mr.
Morrison.

The footman brought in tea, and Mrs. Jack
intimated in a low voice that she was not at
home to anybody; Mr. Morrison hearing it, was

charmed with the idea of intimacy. Then she
quickly possessed herself of his story. It was
not a clever story; outside his business, at
least, Mr. Morrison was not a clever man.
How indeed men, who in conversation, and
sometimes in the conduct of their private lives,
are beyond conception stupid, contrive to amass
money, is a mystery many poor men would like
to solve. It was not a clever story, but it was
as damaging as narrow vindictiveness could make
it, and Mrs. Jack's charity was not proof against
her confidence in people's truth-telling. It was
to the effect that Major Canover had used his
daughter Nelly to lure Mr. Morrison into un-
profitable transactions, and that when he would
part with no more money she had treated him
with incredible rudeness, rudeness which Mr.
Morrison would have thought a lady could not
have employed.

Mildred was deeply shocked. She kept her
eyes lowered as the story proceeded, and once
she passed her hand across them.

"I can't tell you how terribly, how horribly
it distresses me. One never thinks of such
things really happening. It sickens me," she
said with aggrieved innocence. "We Ash-

tons" — Mr. Morrison admired the dignity of the tone — "have our faults, but we are not mean, not dishonest." The cadence woke an echo of some stirring drama: Mr. Morrison felt that life was stately. "Tell me, did any of this happen after her marriage?"

"Well, yes. Shortly after her marriage the Major let me in for a good bit. I might have prosecuted him, but it was n't" — her remark gave him a happy inspiration — "but I thought of your family;" and he was rewarded with a grateful look.

Mildred changed the subject, and they conversed on the iniquity of the world and the beauties of true friendship. When he went he kissed her hand again, and she pressed his warmly, smiling with sorrowful gratitude. She sat down by the tea-table again and meditated for the space of three egg sandwiches. Then she wrote a note to George Ashton asking him to come to see her the next morning.

When he came she received him with great kindness and solemnity, and spoke with reluctant deliberation.

"There's something I feel I ought to tell you, George. It's very much against the grain; I've

argued about it with myself till I felt quite
ill. I implore you not to make too much of
it, but it's not fair not to tell you; you ought
to be on your guard against anything of the
kind happening again. I'd give anything not
to tell you, because it may cause you pain,
and — another thing — nothing could vex me
more than to make mischief between you and
Nelly."

George sighed wearily. "It's about Nelly,
then?"

"Yes, and that's why it's so hard for me. If
you thought for a moment I meant to make
mischief, I should be very unhappy." She faltered a little, and George quickly reassured her.

"There's a Mr. Morrison who used to know
Major Canover."

"I know; I've seen the brute. What has he
to do with Nelly?"

"Unfortunately he has had something to do
with her. Oh, *don't* make too much of it. She
acted thoughtlessly, no doubt, and was influenced
by that old wretch, Major Canover, — I beg your
pardon, dear George; I can't help hating him.
Well, this Mr. Morrson's a business acquaintance
of Jack's, and he came here to see him on busi-

ness, and I had to give him tea. He's a simply dreadful man; it was a mistake of Jack's to let him come to the house." She felt instinctively George's view of Mr. Morrison, and took it for a moment in good faith, I am sure. "Well, he said something about Major Canover and Nelly. I hated to listen, but I thought it better for you to know what he had to say." And she told him Mr. Morrison's story, and somehow, with all her good-natured modifications and excuses, it sounded worse than it had in Mr. Morrison's bald malignancy.

George listened in absolute silence.

"Very well," he said at the end; "the first thing is to do one's best to make Mr. Morrison sorry."

"Now listen to me, George; I knew you would say that, but listen, please." She had foreseen the risk, and was armed against it. She spoke eagerly. It would be such a terrible thing if the affair ended in a vulgar brawl. "If you do that, in the first place you drag me into it. He would say I had betrayed his confidence, and probably have a row with Jack; it would put me in a dreadful position, and I think I don't deserve that, do I? Then he's utterly beneath your

notice. You don't want to fight a cabman who
insults you. He can't do any harm. He swore
he'd told nobody else, and I made him promise
never to do so." Excitement may have confused
her. "Then of course you mustn't believe this
story. I'm afraid poor dear Nelly must have
been indiscreet in some way, or he would never
have dared to say all this, but no doubt it's
exaggerated. Suppose, however, through some
mistake or other there is some ground for what
he says, you would make things a thousand times
worse by making him stand at bay. You see
that?"

"Yes; I suppose it would make things
worse to kick the brute; civilisation's an
infernal thing. But you may be right."

"Promise me you won't speak to him."

"Very well; yes, I promise."

She drew a long breath. "The only thing
to do is this: ask her if this Mr. Morrison
was friends with her; if he lent her father
money, and if she cut him afterwards. If it's
untrue, tell me, and Jack shall make Mr.
Morrison sorry he spoke. If she says it's true,
of course it was all innocent, and she didn't
understand; but I'm afraid you can't complain

of a vulgar man like Mr. Morrison putting a wrong construction on it. Oh, George! I'm really so unhappy about you. I did want your marriage to be happy, and everything seems to go wrong. I hope you'll forgive me if I've ever done anything unwise; I've tried my best."

She was very doleful; but George was abstracted, and murmuring, "Of course; I know," rose to go. He turned back from the door, however, and came towards her.

"Mildred, you've been a very good friend. Forgive me if I don't seem grateful; I really am, but I'm a good deal bothered about things. By the way, do you still want Rowe?"

"Of course we do. But about the rent— it's horrid there should be any question of that sort between us. It doesn't seem much, but we really can't afford more; we've had a good many expenses, and Jack's lost money in the City lately, and then Rowe costs a good deal to keep up. It's either that, or we can't take it. I'm awfully sorry, but we can't help ourselves. How horrid these money questions are!"

"Oh, never mind that; I quite see. I was

only a Jew about it because I was hard up.   I
should hate to have strangers there.   You can
have it all right."

" It's definitely settled then, at the rent I
fixed in my letter; beginning in September? "

" Yes, all right,"

" Dear George, you know we shall care for
it as no strangers will.   Good-bye: do you
really believe I'm your friend? "

There was a sort of melancholy archness in
her look.

" Indeed I do, the best of friends."

A mild emotion of sentimental gratitude is
a very ready resource, when one's other emotions are not agreeable.   George kissed Mildred's
hand as Mr. Morrison had before him.

When he was gone, Mildred had a glow of
angelic feeling.   It had been a painful ordeal,
but she had gone through it bravely, and it is
consoling to have done one's duty, even a duty
of true kindness.   She also felt vaguely that
for practical and sensible people the world is
good.   How foolish to arrange business things
in that haphazard way; but the rent was fixed
now, and she could make terms at her leisure
about improvements and things, and expenses

in keeping up the place ; George could not go back on his word. He was really a dear fellow. It is pleasant, and not wonderful, to know, that after performing her distressing duty, she enjoyed a reaction to great cheerfulness.

CHAPTER XVII

THE CHANCES OF EXPLANATIONS

WHEN George Ashton returned from Scotland, his manner towards his wife was changed. A somewhat frigid politeness was turned into distant kindness, an occasional querulousness gave place to resignation, criticism to indifferent acceptance. He spent most of his time in Half-Moon Street; his whole attitude was more friendly.

But Nelly felt that a stronger barrier than before was between them. She was surely right: the barrier of vague disappointment and irritation by trivial things, a barrier which less sensitive or stronger men surmount with little effort, is a smaller thing than the barrier of passion, — to all men impassable. He looked at his wife and he thought of Madeleine Adair. He saw his wife's romantic beauty, and felt no longer that something was wanting to give it life and a real meaning for him; he felt that another's face shone before it so that it faded to nothingness. Therefore he was evenly kind and kindly indifferent. He made no approaches to her; the distant relation remained unchanged, of course. But he found no fault; there was even something of atonement in his bearing. Nelly was puzzled at first, and then she was conscious that she and he were a thousand miles apart.

Her feeling was like that which comes to us before a thunderstorm, — one of depression and presentiment. Discontent and irritation fell back, as it were, before a larger, more pervading consciousness; she stood face to face with confessed failure, and knew that a consequence, uncertain yet vital, was on its inevitable way. Women see the concrete form of such things more quickly than men, and the idea of separation, though not yet as a certainty, came to the wife first. She did not pity herself. She had been angry, because she fancied that unseen forces she could not face were warring against her, that she could not put fair and straight before her a vague hostility. But now she swept them away in her mind, and told herself that George Ashton and she could never have been happy together for long. "It was an utter mistake." She saw that she had not loved her husband with the love that was in her, a love which could have melted and transformed distaste. She did not blame him; no doubt he had cheated himself. The initial fact that she had married a man whose delicacy was greater than his manfulness she counted against him unconsciously, if at all. She still admired him in a way, still thought he belonged to a higher type than the most of the men she knew. Only he had not understood her; he had exaggerated little things; he had expected great intuition of her, and had shown little of it himself. He had brushed aside her feeling about Mildred Ashton as any common husband might have done, and yet he had required of her to sympathise at once with all his moods and tones. Still, he had never been quite callous or brutal with her, and now he was considerate, like a well-bred host to an unwelcome but invited guest — ah! This life was a very heavy burden to bear; it must come to an end. He oppressed her, and obviously she was something in his way. Well, she had done her best. This is a point of reflection where most of us, men or women, melt

into self-pity; I think it makes my claim for
Nelly's spirit good that she did not pity herself.
She and her husband had made a bargain together; she had done her share as well as she
could, and perhaps he also had tried his best;
but the bargain was bad to both of them.   Her
natural spirit led her to think it was well to
cancel it; the present was a false and very irk-
some position.   But if he wished it to continue,
it was her part to acquiesce and make the best
of things.   After all, what was the alternative?
She thought more kindly than she had, but
wearily still, of Kate and Major Canover and
the old life.

The people who came to see her in these few
days thought she had a headache.   They were
used to fitful gaiety in her and sometimes wild
sayings, and now she was serious and very mildly
mirthful.   The men who imagined they were
flirting with her had misgivings.   She had barely
seen Charlie Skeffington since the autumn; the
sense of shame which the passage between them
had brought insensibly to her had taken the form
of irritation and pointed indifference, while he,
when his irritation was over, felt a sort of inse-
cure self-reproach — he wavered, that is, between

the thought that his superior common sense had been harsh, and the thought that he had not risen to the occasion. But a little time after her husband's return she met Charlie Skeffington in the street, and stopped to speak to him.

"Well, Charlie, still going to the dogs?"

"Yes; still the same old journey. It's taking rather longer than I expected. You all right?"

"Quite, thanks. Poor Charlie, the world's very unkind, is n't it?"

"Everything's beastly," was the dark reply.

Nelly laughed lightly as she nodded and moved on: "Good-bye; try and be good."

George Ashton was conscious, two days after his return, of a difference in his wife. It suited his melancholy mood. If the world must be at cross purposes, and they two must live together, it was well they should do so gravely and decorously. He thought little of his wife now, but he noticed there was less about her to irritate and distract him, and in a way he was grateful. The love for Madeleine Adair gave him a graver and a deeper melancholy. He brooded constantly, and was as unhappy as poor man can be, but in a way it braced him. Two things were clear: he must not see her again, or not for a long time,

and he must order his ways decently in his relations with the rest of the world. He also saw
that the bargain of his marriage was bad, and he
also determined that he would go through with
it, and act fairly towards his wife. The distance
between them he could not break through now,
even if she desired it. That was too much, impossible. By-and-bye, as time went on, that
might be remedied. Meanwhile he would try to
understand, or at least, while it was impossible
for him to think of anything but one thing, he
must study to be kind.

Nelly, of course, speculated vaguely in her
mind on the possibility of something having
happened in Scotland to cause the change in her
husband. She was conscious that something
more than had been was between them, and the
idea of another woman came to her inevitably,
as to a woman. But she dismissed the idea of
Scotland: her thoughts turned to Lady Tremayne. She remembered Mildred's suggestion,
but she did not believe there was an actual passion of love between them. Probably they had
sentimentalised together — ugh! it was contemptible to her — and Lady Tremayne had
sorrowfully impressed on him his duty to his

wife. She hated Lady Tremayne. The natures,
the attitudes to life, of the two women were antipathetic. Nelly thought that Lady Tremayne
probably regarded her from a serene height, and
pitied her, and pitied George, and talked to him
sympathetically, and was so clever, so insidious.
. . . Mildred Ashton became unimportant by
comparison; and when she came to Half Moon
Street on the day of Mr. Morrison's entertain-
ment at lunch, Nelly, albeit cold as ever, was
more equable, less nervous in her manner towards
her. Mildred noticed this, and noticed also
George's greater kindness and consideration for
his wife, and when she went away murmured
softly to Nelly, "I'm so glad."

"What about?"

"About many things, dear;" she smiled kindly
patronage and gave no time for another question.
Her face was thoughtful as she went down the
stairs.

Then came Mr. Morrison's disclosure and the
sad necessity of telling it to George. As he
walked back to his house after the interview he
was utterly miserable at first, and then intensely
angry. He had been doing his best — I fear he
pitied himself — to be kind to his wife; her ex-

istence wrecked his life, or prevented its salvation, but she was not responsible for that, and he had tried with all his might to be just. And now came this business. Things were really impossible. It was all so vulgar, so sordid. It was worse: in his view, for a woman to get money from a man by means of her beauty and graces, within commonly innocent bounds, was very nearly as bad as if the bounds were not commonly innocent. That greasy ruffian must have had something to go upon; he could not have invented the whole thing. And for his wife — it was damnation! The Ashtons had been honourable people for centuries; the fact had always given him a superiority — surely not ridiculous — over those more highly placed who used their position sordidly. His wife had done this for her rogue of a father, certainly; that hardly mattered. She knew he would have given the scamp twice the money, — ten times the money, if the other had been the alternative. That was the sort of environment he had made for himself; he might have made — of that he would not think.

He found Major Canover come to lunch, who greeted him cheerily.

"Glad to see you, my boy. How well you're looking! Scotland's done marvels for you."

George sat almost in silence during lunch, and when the butler had finally left the room, turned abruptly to his father-in-law.

"You know a man called Morrison?"

"Morrison — Morrison? Of course, yes. Haven't seen him for some time, though. Vulgar fellow. Those fellows, you know, are all very well for a time; then they show the cloven hoof. Morrison was like that: got all he could — in a social way, you know — out of me, and then turned round."

"I see. The social advantages included the society of my wife?"

"Eh — what? My good fellow, I don't understand you."

"I ask you if it is a fact that you had commercial dealings with this Morrison, and that while they were in course of transaction my wife met him — I remember you being good enough to take her to dinner with him — was friendly with him, in fact, and that when he turned round, as you say, she cut him, as she should have done the second time she met him?"

"Good God, George, what a ridiculous fuss

about nothing! Upon my soul, I never heard anything like it in my life. Upon my soul, never! What do you mean, sir, by such a tone?"

" Do you owe this fellow money, and did he refuse to lend you more?"

" I decline to answer impertinent questions. And I decline to allow myself to be insulted at your table." The Major's dignity was secure for a moment and it had no longer strain.

" You can obviate that for the future," George said; " at present I 'll obviate it myself," and he rose and walked out of the room.

The Major turned a boiling face to his daughter.

" This husband of yours is simply the most cantankerous brute I 've ever met. Mean brute too, or I would n't — by Jove he 'd make a saint mad."

" It 's no use abusing him, father."

" Then what did he mean by his infernal questions? What 's he got to do with Morrison? Damn Morrison. What 's Morrison got to do with you?"

" I suppose some kind friend has told George some idiotic story. But for him to speak like that — it's the last straw." She dashed away the tears from her eyes. "Morrison must have talked about me. That's your fault, father, if you've borrowed money from him and not paid. Yes, it is, but it's no use talking about that. If George understands me so little, we'd better separate."

"H'm," said the Major. "He'll have to make you an allowance, besides the settlements. I suppose you'd come back and live with us. Well, well; it might be best if he goes on like this."

And after a few fatherly consolations Major Canover took his leave, banging the hall door with a final bang.

George came back to the dining-room, and Nelly sat up very straightly and looked at him indifferently.

"You were friends with this Morrison?"

"You know I was: in a way, yes."

"Did you know your father was borrowing money from him?"

Of course Nelly had known that some such connection would necessarily subsist between Mr. Morrison and Major Canover for them to be friends. She had hardly thought definitely of it when she was asked to dine with him; for years she had been accustomed to meet Major Canover's lending friends. To have quarrelled with Mr. Morrison for not lending money to the Major, or being unpleasant about money lent, was a meanness of which she could not have thought. Nor would she have made herself amiable to a man she fairly disliked for any sordid reason. She was easily pleased, and had rather liked Mr. Morrison; and, when he had assumed on his money to try to force an intimacy, had dismissed him without hesitation. All this is certain. But it is also certain that her husband's question could only be answered honestly in the affirmative, and her spirit rose, and she said:

"I dare say he was. I utterly refuse to be catechised about it. I have nothing to do with it."

So she did not tell her husband why she had cut Mr. Morrison.

A thought struck her, and she asked:

"Did Mildred tell you this story? No, I don't want to hear; of course you'd defend her. You remember they dine here to-morrow with the Tremaynes and the Careys? No; I won't put it off. It's only one more annoyance."

George hardly listened. He had turned away in disgust and left his wife to her tears. In the hall he was met by a note. It was from Lady Tremayne.

"Madeleine Adair came yesterday to stay with me. She wants to see you very much and at once, and I think you had better come. Maurice will be all the evening at the House, and we shall be alone. Come about half-past nine if you possibly can. C. T."

CHAPTER XVIII

AN END OF FOLLY

WHEN George Ashton was gone, a blight seemed to fall upon the frankness and the gaiety of Glenburn. Madeleine talked at meals and was sometimes almost boisterously bright. But when the others talked apart she was listless; she shut herself in her room for most of the day; she was pale and excused herself from singing, to which indeed she was never pressed. Tommy Tucker was melancholy; he talked less cheerily though more cleverly than before; in a few days he went away. Mrs. Adair was troubled, anxious, more maternal. But the lowest depths of visible dejection were reached by Bob Adair. He had fits of silence and watched his sister when she looked away from him. He cursed English habits and swore at his valet, after the manner of simple man in distress.

Sometimes Madeleine looked at Fanny when they were alone and seemed to hesitate; but she never talked to Fanny of what ailed her. She was fond of her brother's wife, and in better times had been merry and seemed to be intimate with her; she did not recognise in her that certainty of response which may bring complete confidence in such a sorrow as hers. Perhaps she felt that Mrs. Adair would have been more reticent than she herself was disposed by nature to be; an idea of race may have influenced her: in any case she did not speak. If she had had any doubt of George Ashton's love for her, the wish to speak would, I suppose, not have existed at all. But she accepted the idea of his love frankly, and longed, on impulse, to tell her mind. Once she whispered to her brother as she kissed him; "Oh, Bob, Bob, I 'm so unhappy," and he hugged her: "Darling Maddo, I would give all my life to get what you want," and he was French enough to let his eyes be wet. Then suddenly she drew herself up and put her hands on his shoulders and looked into his face. "Bob, I must see him once and say something to him and then never see him again. I shall go to London for a day or two."

Bob's eyes dropped and he thought. Then he looked at her again.

"Maddo, you know I only want your happiness. I would care nothing what the world said in a different case. If you wanted to marry somebody — somebody not your equal socially, say, and if he were a good fellow, I would n't say a word. But this is different, utterly. You want to see him —"

"I must speak to him, Bob, it is justice to me, and justice to him. Only once."

"I see — I know what you feel; you may be right. But will you promise me you'll never see him again, — never try to see him, that is?"

"On my honour."

"Shall I ask him down here for a day?"

"It had better be in London. I shall go to Lady Tremayne for a day or two. She's a friend of his; she can arrange for us to meet."

"Will you tell her?"

"I don't know, I don't know. I shall see; I may. Don't ask me about that. But I shall go to her. Will you tell Fan, Bob? Oh, Bob, your poor Maddo's very unhappy, but she's going to be good and not worry everybody else."

She smiled wearily on him and he went to find his wife. As he went he reflected. It is not in human nature to feel sorrow for another and not to stretch at hope: Bob Adair reflected — and her last words helped him — that everything changes in this world, even the first real love of a girl. Then he smiled, as being near to a paradox. Poor darling Maddo! But everything changes. He spoke reticently to his wife, for he too felt that she might not wholly understand his sister, would not feel, as he felt, that her longing for one plain speech was right and true to herself. But he could not ignore her knowledge entirely.

"Do you think she is wise to go, Bob?"

"Wise? Well, yes, if there can be wisdom in it at all. Better shake hands with him again and say good-bye definitely. Vagueness frets one in these things. Yes, I think she is wise."

"Bob, you know I like your friend, and I don't blame him now. But are you quite sure, quite sure you can speak for him as you can for yourself."

Bob shot a curious glance at his wife. Women — the thought darted through his brain — are strangely possessive; he adored his wife,

yes, yes; but she did not know what Maddo
meant to him. That he could be careless of
her!

"That hardly needs an answer, dearest. If I
did not know George to be an absolutely honourable man, do you suppose I would let her speak
to him again, now I know what I know? If I
thought for one moment he had made love to
her, tried to make her love him, do you know
what I would do?" He dropped his hand to
his side, a little final gesture. "We won't think
any more of that, please. But all the honour in
the world won't prevent two people caring for
one another, from being blind. Blind, yes, and
we too. It was we who were fools, Fan; we
should have seen, and I shall never forgive
myself. But everything passes, you know,
everything; and Maddo will be happy again one
day. As to her seeing George once more, that
is best for both of them. Your stage brothers
— bah! your ranting melodramatic brothers —
would sacrifice that to a sense of propriety, I
suppose. I value Maddo's wish more than that.
But I would n't allow it, dear, if I did n't know
that George Ashton is delicate and honourable
in every point, and if I did n't trust Maddo as I

would trust the Mother of God." He turned
away abruptly and left the room.

There are other emotions than love that play
tricks with our heads. Bob Adair, who had
been bred a Catholic, had long smiled indifferently at Christianity; yet he had spoken in
absolute sincerity, being moved to passion by
any semblance of doubt of his sister. Mrs.
Adair sat and wondered awhile, dimly compre-
hending that there was more in her husband
than a sweet temper and a frivolous manner.
She was very gentle to him and to Madeleine
when they met later, with almost an appeal in
her eyes. They were very silent, and Madeleine
hung, for a moment, on Fanny's neck when she
went to bed.

Two days later, Madeleine went to London.
Lady Tremayne supposed the girl was bored
in Scotland, and wished to shop and go to
theatres, and was surprised and interested by
her quietude and gravity when they met. She
arrived in the late afternoon, and talked alone
with Lady Tremayne gravely and intimately
about her father and her brother's marriage
and the life in Scotland. She was asked about
George Ashton's visit; and "I like him very

much indeed," was all she said, and she changed
the subject shortly. Lady Tremayne wondered
a little, and dismissed the wonder. Length of
acquaintance had given an intimacy of Christian names; intimacy of affection had been
mostly on impulsive Madeleine's side; but
Clara Tremayne, who was in tune for affection,
grew rapidly, as they talked, to feel that the
girl, whose mother she remembered with
admiration and whose father with real esteem,
had always been dear to her, and was one to
love.

At dinner Madeleine brightened and amused
Sir Maurice with quaint, clever questions on
politics, with stories of her neighbours in
Scotland, and stories of Bob Adair. She sang
him a song or two after dinner, to his delight,
in a voice in which Lady Tremayne detected
an under-note of weariness or sadness.

When Sir Maurice went to the House, Madeleine's manner changed again. She talked
pensively, and wanted to go to bed early.
Passing by her door soon afterwards, Lady
Tremayne heard a sob, and knocked softly and
was bidden, by a stifled voice, to enter . . .

" Dear Clara, you are very good to me.

Yes; I'll tell you. It's a stupid old story. Lots of people have been as unhappy before, perhaps. But I'm as unhappy as I know how to be. I care for somebody whom I must only see once more in my life."

Lady Tremayne stroked the hair of the girl as she knelt. "My poor darling girl. Can't I help? I would do anything. May I know who it is? I don't want to, but I might be able to help." As she spoke a presentiment came upon her.

"I meant to tell you, Clara . . . I would n't speak of him when we talked before dinner . . . "

A sigh which was not interpreted escaped Lady Tremayne, and that was all. What had been her feeling towards George Ashton? She told herself now that it had been affectionate, pitying, tender, not of passion at all. But she felt for a moment very lonely. She did not accuse him; he had not been bound to her; it was all very natural. Here was a beautiful, bright girl — she stroked Madeleine's hair again. Remember she had been schooled to sorrow, the mild grey sorrow that is absence of joy, had met with little response. George Ashton had been

in love with his wife, and she had not, she
thought, cared very deeply. Why should she
care now? These two poor things needed pity.
She did not believe that George Ashton had
acted otherwise than blindly. It was all a pitiful
accident. She had been his friend for years, and
would be his friend now. What did she matter?
Madeleine looked up after a silence and saw her
friend was crying softly, and took the tears to
herself. Clara Tremayne gave her the comfort
that women use.

George Ashton came at half-past nine the
next evening with a set, unsmiling face, and
walked quickly into the drawing-room to find
Sir Maurice Tremayne standing before the fireplace and explaining a Government Bill. He
had been told at the last moment that he need
not go to the House till half-past eleven. He
wondered a little why George Ashton should
have come more than anyone else, but accepted
the situation and plied him with questions about
his wife's health, his mother's health, and the
health of that charming cousin of his, Mrs. Jack
Ashton. So for two hours three poor people
sat grimacing politely while the suave old gentle-

man prosed. George stayed him out without excuse, and when he was gone Lady Tremayne left the room without a word, and Madeleine Adair told George Ashton what he knew, and said good-bye to him for ever.

"I know you care for me. I wanted to hear you say so, and to tell you I care for you, so that we may have something to remember. You know, we must not talk together again."

So much of the speech of the girl may be told a generation whose sentiment is mostly for other things. Who knows what this man and this woman, so placed, must have said to one another? Who, knowing, would care to tell it to the world? I cannot say if our mothers would have approved such speech from a girl to a man who was married: likely not, indeed. But I think the ethical import of it has been explained sufficiently by Bob Adair.

Lady Tremayne, sitting hopelessly in the next room, heard, without remembering she was hearing, voices talking earnestly, once and again impetuously. She heard weeping and the door open, and she went out on to the staircase. She followed George Ashton into the hall.

"God bless you, George, and make you strong.

George, remember, it is not the fault of your wife."

"No, I remember. You have been my best friend. Good night."

He hardly looked at her, and walked quickly away from the house. As he left it, it chanced that Mr. and Mrs. Jack Ashton, returning from supper, it being about one o'clock, passed by in a cab and saw him. Their passing reminds me that sentiment may run riot.

CHAPTER XIX.

MENDING A MISTAKE.

ABOUT ten the next morning, George Ashton received a note from Lady Tremayne. " She has gone back to Scotland ; braver than I could have hoped. Do you be brave too. Your friend, C. T." I will do him justice; his first feeling on reading it was one of shame, that he or his sorrow should be mentioned. What was he in comparison with Madeleine Adair, fool and brute that he was? But such an emotion, the result perhaps of an artificial attitude, passes quickly when a man's feelings are truly troubled, and George Ashton settled into hopeless misery. One idea, a dumb final negation, obsessed his brain altogether, and the hours passed by like years, but without count. He could not even go out to his club, — why does London lead always to bathos? — but sat in his den effortless. He noticed that his wife did not come to lunch, and was glad to need no excuse not to eat. He did not even drink that day, but later, having slept not at all the night before, fell asleep and dreamed of the first night at Glenburn and the merry dinner.

Nelly also had not slept and lay most of the day in sheer physical incapacity, with her head crushing in upon itself. She went to Victoria Road in the afternoon, and finding several people there, talked rather wildly, inviting Kate, who was inclined to snub her, to corroborate absurd anecdotes of their childhood. "You're going out too much," said Kate, when they parted; "you look quite ill. Father's in a dreadful state," she added in a lower voice, and Nelly answered that that was all right now; it was all over.

Frank Carey and his wife, most charitable of people, were forced to admit afterwards that never was there a duller little dinner-party than that at Half Moon Street that evening. Mrs. Carey, a little witch-like woman, with a very sweet manner and an infinite store of appreciation and ready response, had been accustomed to count George Ashton of her most interesting friends; to-night he smiled fatuously when she

spoke and made remarks she remembered he
had made at other times. There seemed to be
an understanding between him and Lady Tremayne, on his other side, not to talk at all.

Neither Frank Carey, a man who liked an
argument, nor Sir Maurice Tremayne, who liked
to give information, could make anything con-
versationally of Nelly; she had a lightness that
was patently artificial; her eyes wandered con-
tinually to Mildred Ashton or Lady Tremayne,
and turned away abruptly but with the thread
of talk only nominally sustained. Mr. and
Mrs. Digby Fleetwood, the fifth pair of diners,
were people who looked conversational but
talked very little; a brilliant table did not suffer
by their presence; a dull one was not lightened.
Jack Ashton was prepared to work for his dinner by a reasonable amount of lip service, but
he was afraid of Mrs. Carey, who indeed regarded him as a man-ox, and Mrs. Fleetwood
and he economised topics very carefully. Mildred, as always, was very much at her ease, and
ate, as was her custom, a very substantial dinner; but even she seemed a trifle preoccupied.
She listened placidly, with an occasional pleasant smile of intelligence, to Sir Maurice, who

turned to her from Nelly; Mr. Fleetwood and Lady Tremayne imitated Jack Ashton's economy. Certainly it was a very dull dinner.

Mildred waited for Nelly outside the door, and taking her arm affectionately walked very slowly up stairs, so that they were somewhat behind the others.

"Isn't dear Lady Tremayne looking sweet?" she said. "She had an at-home or something last night, didn't she?"

"I don't know," said Nelly. By this time the others were inside the drawing-room and Mildred and she half up the stairs.

"Why, I saw you coming away about one," said Mildred. "Jack and I were going by in a hansom. At least George was coming out, — just inside the door, — and there was somebody behind him I thought must be you."

"I wasn't there."

"Weren't you? what a stupid mistake of mine. I suppose it wasn't George then; I didn't see very well."

And Mildred no doubt dismissed the trivial matter from her mind. But on Nelly the casual information had an exaggerated effect. All the day she had brooded, so far as her headache allowed, on her whole relation with her husband, on what he had said about Mr. Morrison, and above all on his manner of saying it. She had been maddened to think that while she was trying, trying with all her might, to do her share of the bargain and not to irritate or annoy him, he should come carelessly with a vulgar insinuation. She said to herself that she was wretched, and she thought longingly of her childhood and so had gone to Victoria Road. The thought of Lady Tremayne also was continuously present with her; her husband's silly sentiment for this woman had made him utterly indifferent to her own feelings. She had eaten almost nothing, and worried herself incessantly all day long. And now she learned that while she had been tossing in her bed and crying, he had been philandering with Lady Tremayne; that he, of course, who could bring a stupid accusation against his wife, was so superior to vulgar interpretations that he could stay alone with Lady Tremayne till one. She remembered that Sir Maurice had complained at dinner of the twelve o'clock rule having been suspended the night before and of his having been kept at the house till three. Of course George had been talking sentiment, probably receiving sympathy about his wife.

She talked at random to Mrs. Carey and Mrs. Fleetwood, and after a time rose suddenly and went to where Lady Tremayne was sitting alone, Mildred having risen to put down her coffee cup.

"Was George with you last night?" She asked abruptly.

Lady Tremayne was annoyed; her mind flew to Madeleine Adair, but she acquitted Nelly of significance.

"Yes; he came in after dinner."

"I only ask because I've seen very little of him of late, and I want to know how you think he is. You had a good opportunity of judging, as he stayed till one."

Nelly hardly knew what she was saying: her head was in agony and an expression of blind resentment was a necessary physical relief. She had not meant to speak so plainly. But Lady Tremayne naturally thought it was vulgar jealousy, very vulgarly expressed.

"I don't think he's very well," she said frigidly, and turned with a remark to Mildred, who was now standing before them with a pleasant social

smile. Like three other foolish people, Lady
Tremayne had been sleepless and without food.
Her nerves were over-strained; she had begun
to think she had done more for George Ashton
than woman should be asked to do. And now
to be involved in a vulgar recrimination with
that jealous girl was the last straw. She sat in
silence for a little time, but very soon after the
men arrived rose and pleaded a sudden headache and ill health and went away with Sir
Maurice, who in fact was extremely glad to go.

When George returned from the door, Mrs.
Jack with a nod beckoned him to where she had
moved apart from the others, and they sat down
side by side.

"Oh, George," she said in a low voice, "I'm
in such trouble. I could cry with vexation.
I've made mischief; I don't think anybody
could have foreseen it, but I'm miserable about
it."

He leaned wearily back in his chair beside
her. "I don't suppose it will make any difference," he said; "I'm sure you didn't mean to.
Don't bother to talk about it."

"But I must, George, it might put it right.
You know Jack and I were going past Lowndes

Street last night and saw you come out." He sat up and leaned back again. "Yes, that is, I saw you, and thought it was Nelly standing behind you, just inside. Of course I'm not idiot enough to think there's any reason in the world why you should not have been there — she's such a sweet woman, Lady Tremayne. But I mentioned it casually to Nelly and she seemed to mind. I can't tell you how vexed I am; it was simply a mistake: oh, George, I'm so frightfully sorry."

"But what in heaven's name is the objection? There was no reason you should not have mentioned it even if you had n't thought Nelly was there. I don't understand."

"Of course, George, of *course:* it's so absurd. But Nelly — I think she must be ill or something — made a complaint to Lady Tremayne, and I'm afraid that's why she went away."

She stopped suddenly and looked anxiously at him. His pale face flushed and grew paler, and his eyes looked hard, and he set his mouth.

"Very well; I see. It was n't your fault; you were quite right to tell me."

"I thought I'd better. I am so sorry."

"You were perfectly right. I'm grateful to you for telling me."

She looked at him with affectionate concern.
His brain was at a dead-lock of anger; the emotions of the day centred in that.   That his last
meeting with Madeleine should be vulgarised
in such a way, that Clara Tremayne, who had
stood such a true and delicate friend to him,
should be met with this vulgar annoyance, that
the sacredness, as he thought it, of his love
should be so invaded, maddened him.   George
Ashton could have struck his wife then, and I
suppose there are cynics who would say that if
they had been alone, and he had done so, the
upshot of things might have been better.

When the Careys and the Fleetwoods went,
Jack Ashton looked at his wife with a yawn
in his eyes, but she sat down again placidly.
George spoke to Nelly from the door: " I wish
to speak to you for a moment."   She went list-
lessly towards him.   Jack looked at his wife
again to no purpose.

" You said something insulting to Lady Tremayne? "   George spoke in a half whisper.

" I remarked on your being there. If there
was no harm in that, there was no harm in my
mentioning it, I suppose."

" You insulted her and drove her out of my

house. She is my best friend; she has done more for me than a million people like you could do for anyone. That is the end, Nelly. I've done my best, but this is too much. We must separate."

Nelly raised her voice. "Thank God, at last! I take you at your word, George." She turned to the others. "You may as well hear; it will make it irrevocable. George has offered me a separation, and I have accepted it."

Jack looked forlornly at the door. But Mildred spoke with quiet decision.

"George, will you go with Jack to your den? I have something to say to Nelly."

"I wish to hear nothing on this topic," Nelly said.

"You can hardly refuse to hear me. I won't keep you long."

George and Jack went downstairs to the smoking-den. Jack cleared his throat and spoke.

"I say, old chap, you know, I'm beastly sorry —"

"You needn't talk about it. It's no use, and I'm sure you haven't the remotest idea what to say. We'll play a hand at picquet."

"Oh, I say, you know, wouldn't it be, wouldn't it look —"

"Nonsense.   There'll be time for a deal."

And so the two men, Jack very much relieved, sat down to picquet.

In the drawing-room Nelly and Mrs. Jack stood near the door.

"What is it you want to say?"

"Nelly, you're ill to-night, hysterical.   You couldn't have meant —"

"It's useless to talk about that."

"Don't be a silly child; it's ridiculous —"

"I decline to let you talk to me in that way. I shall go to bed."

She moved towards the door, but Mildred caught hold of her wrist, and Nelly, feeling a strength twice her own in the grasp, stood still. They looked at one another, both fair to see in their ways, the one romantic, fevered, contemptuous, the other sleek, healthy, determined; waywardness and despair, common sense and prosperity.

Nelly moved away from the door, and Mildred let go her wrist.

"Now, listen to me.   I don't want to interfere. I speak for the best.   You are ill to-night, and if you do anything rash you'll repent it to-morrow.   Better make it up now: to-morrow you'll both feel foolish when you repent. I don't want to meddle, but I 've done my best always to make peace, and I must do my best now."

Nelly turned round and flashed upon her.

" I 'll tell you once for all what I think. You 've been my enemy all along; you 've done everything you could to make mischief. You 're clever enough to do it in a way I could n't meet, but don't suppose I did n't see. I used to hate you, but now it 's all over, I simply think you 're contemptible. But don't imagine you 've had any influence, it would have happened without you just the same. But now you 've got what you want, and we need n't meet again."

Mildred flushed and half clenched her hand. " How dare you? " she said, but recovered herself at once. " But I don't care for a vulgar quarrel. I shall forget what you said; you could n't have meant it; it 's too insane. As for this silly separation, I suppose you 'll decide on it to-night, and in a week I shall hear you 've made it up, and then I shall say ' I told you so,' and we shall be friends again."

" Wait and see," said Nelly, very firmly, and walked to the other end of the room.

Mildred shook her head despairingly, and

went down-stairs. She entered the smoking-room with the face of an angel despondent over human errors, and went up to George's chair, and put her hand on his shoulder.

"Dear George," she said in a low voice, "I've done my best. I tried to make things right. Nelly spoke very cruelly to me — " she turned away her head — " but I don't mind that. I'm so utterly miserable about it. Tell me, George, you don't blame me for anything."

He stood up and smiled at her. " Of course not, Mildred, you 've been a real friend. Don't be too sad about it. People make mistakes, you know, and by far the best thing is to face them."

But Jack Ashton and his wife went away very sorrowfully, Jack saying good-bye with portentous solemnity, Mildred with a lingering grasp of her hand. Then George went back to the drawing-room, and Nelly stood up as he came in. As he saw the utterly sad but brave look in her eyes, he felt sorry for her unhappiness. The thought of Madeleine Adair flashed upon him. It was wise Nelly and he should part; it was best for both of them.

"I beg your pardon, Nelly, if I spoke rudely to you. We agree to part, and we 'll part friends, if you will. I shall go out early to-morrow. I think you'd better ask your father to take you into the country for a few days while everything's arranged. Good-bye."

Nelly looked at him hard and stood silently. Then, " Good-bye," she said with an even voice, and turned away, and he left the room, to think I suppose, of Madeleine Adair, whom he should never see again, the thought of whom made this parting welcome.

Meantime Mildred and Jack drove home in silence, save for an occasional expression of regret. But when they were home, she turned back at the foot of the staircase.

" All these scenes have quite worn me out. It's no use making oneself ill. I know you'd like some supper. Go and forage like a good boy: there are some plover's eggs, I know, and some cold chicken. And you might bring up a small bottle of champagne. I'll go to my darling while you get it."

> "When we are scourged, we kiss the rod
> Resigning to the will of God,"

— but I am sure Mildred Ashton thought she was sorry.

CHAPTER XX

A HAPPY ENDING

So George Ashton and Nelly his wife were separated. Mrs. Jack the morning after her fruitless intervention in the cause of peace sent an early note to George, begging him to relieve her anxiety; had they not really made it up after all? An answer came back at once to the effect that Nelly was already gone to her father, with whom she was going out of town, and that the decision was irrevocable. Then Mrs. Jack, in spite of her weariness of the night before, took the next train to Rowe, determining that the only immediate scope for her kindness was to break the news to old Mrs. Ashton.

She seemed to have reconciled herself on the way to the wisdom of the separation, for when Mrs. Ashton was for going at once to town and doing her utmost to effect a reconciliation, Mildred argued, gently but very firmly, against

any such action. She pointed out that she had
seen a great deal of George and Nelly, and
could judge, and that, having striven against
such a conclusion with all her might, was convinced they would never live happily together.
Finally she confessed, since the truth, however
painful, could no longer be glossed over, that
Nelly was utterly unworthy of her husband.
Mildred had thought so in the beginning, but
had done her best all along — in the face of
continual ingratitude and even insult — to be
Nelly's good friend. Facts, however, were too
strong. Nelly had flirted — a vulgar word
which Mildred disliked; she would not use a
harsher — in a most dreadful way with several
men, especially with Lord Skeffington. And
Mrs. Jack was afraid it could not be called
simply girlish light-headedness and want of
good taste; she told, with great reluctance,
the painful story of Mr. Morrison, which indeed
indicated to Mrs. Ashton a horrible atmosphere
from which, at all costs, her poor boy must be
taken. So in the end she wrote sympathy and
not remonstrance to her son, and shortly afterwards a deed of separation was made.

This fact has, I suppose, the air of a climax.

But if you will bear with a fondness for old
fashions, I should like to tell you what has
happened to these people since, and how they
are placed at present.

It is, as I write, but two years since the last
event mentioned, and the sage has warned us
to call no man happy before his death. But
it is my sincere conviction that for the most
part the people introduced to you in these pages
have enjoyed or are enjoying as much happiness
as may be reasonably expected in a world of
compromise and incompleteness. The wayward and the over-sensitive are not likely to be
so continuously happy as they who are eupeptic
and content with simple things, who use appropriate means to ends and are in harmony with
their environment. Allowing for that difference,
I can see no excessive hardship for George or
Nelly Ashton, for Lady Tremayne, or for Madeleine Adair.

After his separation from his wife George went
to stay with his mother at the dower-house at
Rowe. He walked about the place and read a
great deal, and sat still for hours without reading.
He never spoke of his wife to Mrs. Ashton, but
he tended her constantly, reading to her in the

evenings, talking to her of old days. And she
was perhaps happier at heart than she had been
for many a day, secure, as she thought, in her
son's whole love; she clung to it almost passion-
ately, and perhaps with prescience. For in a
few months she died. Then George went abroad,
and was lost to his friends for some months. He
felt quite alone now, and his impulses clamoured
to console him. He appeared in London in the
winter, haggard and feverish, and men at his
club shook their heads over his habits. Only
one vice was known of him; he had not the true
gambler's nature, and gave up high stakes when
his irritations were settled once for all, and the
habit of light love had left him; he was never
drunk, but he drank continuously. By and bye
he broke down, and had an attack of brain fever,
and Mildred Ashton came up from the country
to nurse him, and when he was convalescent she
took him back with her to Rowe. Since his
recovery he has lived mostly in the Temple,
reading a good deal, and even writing fitfully,
going hardly at all into the world, save for an
occasional meal at his club, or for a quiet dinner
with the Jack Ashtons when they are in town.
He stays at Rowe sometimes, the ice having been

broken in his convalescence. Everybody praises
Mildred's angelic kindness towards him, and
indeed he owes her a good deal. He is much
under her eye, and increasingly under her direction. She visits him in the Temple, and orders
his affairs, about which he is listless, and, thanks
to her, he lives well within his income. He has, to
do him justice, shown her a gratitude she appreciated, having promised to leave his money to her
boy, — her elder boy, for Providence had very
properly entrusted her with another, — and having given her all his mother's jewels, save one he
kept for a wedding present.

The habit of wine of course recurred, and he
is unlikely to live a great number of years; still,
he is never indecorous in that respect, and his
monitress has, with sighs, abandoned that par-
ticular reform. As was inevitable, also, he has
occasionally amused himself in another way.
He has seen his wife a few times in the street,
and passed her with a smile and a conventional
salutation. When people talked scandal of her
a little time ago, he rejected angrily a hinted
advice that he should try for a divorce, and in
this he was supported by Mrs. Jack, who speaks
with great kindness and pity of Nelly Ashton.

A motive which might have prompted him has
been removed. Certainly George Ashton is not
unhappy. He amuses himself in his own way;
his intellect still serves him to some purpose,
and he knows how to keep himself in common
cheerfulness. And I question if his life be more
unworthy than that of most idlers whose ideals
have been disappointed.

Nelly returned a little time after the separation to Victoria Road, and faced the world. Her
own world, indeed, was for the most part sympathetic. It was inclined to rejoice at what had
happened. The men of it found no reserved
host there to interrupt the freedom of their talk;
the women, or most of them, were pleased by
an essential equality of position. Her settlements had been ample in the circumstances; she
refused an allowance her husband offered her in
addition. This somewhat aggrieved Major Canover; he intervened as a correspondent with
George Ashton, and presently his good humour
was restored. So the dinners in Victoria Road
were better than they had been. The Canovers
and Nelly, however, spent most of the year
abroad, where the Major encounters fewer men

who have shown the cloven hoof; Dieppe sees
them often, Monte Carlo often, Boulogne, when
funds are lower, sometimes. As times went by,
Nelly regained her old spirits. It is impossible
for such a nature to be depressed for ever: it
must laugh or it must die. She had thought to
live on a higher plane than of old, and had found
(she told herself) the new life a cheat; now she
was frankly where she had been; her thoughts
are bitter, it may be, from time to time, but it is
certain that she is merry and amused. She is
more beautiful than ever, and still with the beauty
of a girl. Many men admire her to distraction;
some, as of old, are her true friends. When her
husband dies, which will be probably before she
is much over thirty, she is certain to marry again,
some easy-going worldling, it is likely, who will
be kind and give and take. She remembers her
husband more faintly every month; it is impossible for a sentimentalist to say she is unhappy.
Potentialities there are in her which have been
half evoked and laid aside; actualities of pleasure she has in very reasonable measure.

George Ashton and Lady Tremayne meet but
very seldom now. Both may feel a certain shame,

he for a vague disloyalty, she for a vague exces-
siveness of friendship. She thinks of him with
sentiment, no doubt, and you know there is a
pleasure, after a while, in some sorts of retro-
spective sorrow. She reads more than ever, and
since Sir Maurice's restoration to activity, has
hunted again, and again looks very young for
her years. She also has friendships, possibly
sentimental friendships. Is there hypocrisy in
that? Here is a woman of brain and heart to
whom life has offered little of strong reality.
Who is called upon to complain of sentimental
friendships?

There is a jingle by a great poet which says
our sighing ends not in dying, and Madeleine
Adair is alive. When she went back to Glenburn she was desolate and physically ill. But
she was very young and as the weeks went by
the crying need in her for gaiety was forced into
an outlet. She began to joke, quietly and not
excitedly, with her brother ; she began, as of old,
to tease Fanny Adair. Towards the end of the
autumn Bob began to think that a change of
scene would make Glenburn more delightful in
the next spring, and all of them went to France,

and spent Christmas in Paris. There were old
friends for Madeleine, old schoolfellows become
young wives, her mother's intimates who petted
her, sympathy and regard. She brightened
daily; George Ashton became a definite epi-
sode of the past. But Madeleine Adair could
play no tricks of maidenly self-deception. " I
was in love with George Ashton," she thought,
a year after she had seen him last; "I was true
in that, and I shall not forget it, and I shall
never be ashamed of it. The feeling has grown
dim, somehow. I don't understand; it was a
true feeling, and I am not shallow. Perhaps if
I saw him again I should feel as I did."

Perhaps, yes. It is the rule of our poor being
that intimacies, even passions, that are quickly
formed, do fade quickly if their visible stimulus
is taken away. If Madeleine had married George
Ashton or even if they had been much together,
doubtless her love would have lived. She did
not see him again until she was married, and
then, for a shake of the hand and common conversation only. As it was, her love lived in
memory; it was never falsified or betrayed.

To the surprise of his friends, who are everybody, Tommy Tucker went to South Africa

last autumn, as somebody's secretary. An uncle, who had prophesied good of Tommy, and hated him accordingly in his idleness, was triumphant enough to put down Tommy for a comfortable sum in his will, and obliging enough to die in the following spring, whereon Tommy promptly returned to England. His first visit was to Glenburn. He did not pester Madeleine at all. The old intimacy was re-established on a deeper foundation, it appeared. They were very good friends, and in their youth, and it was spring again, and for all that the world had laughed at him, there was something in Tommy Tucker that made contempt impossible. He was wittier than of old; he proved his brains daily, and, Madeleine thought — and had been told by Fanny, who had tact enough to tell her once only — he had proved his character a year ago. So he asked her to marry him and was accepted, and was transformed, showing signs of a Tommy Tucker who might do something in the world. She may have been touched by his constancy; I think she believed she cared for him truly, and thought that the past was past, and here was some happiness before her. Surely none

but the stupidest of sentimentalists would
reproach her, and even he could not deny
that she is happy herself and spreads happiness round her, and has made Tommy
Tucker, whom everybody likes, the happiest
of husbands.

All its district of Hampshire rejoices that Rowe
at length has really hospitable occupiers. Jack
Ashton and his wife live there most of the year,
Jack going to town occasionally. They come to
London for the season, and pay a few visits, but
are in their element and glory as the hosts of
Rowe, where they have the moral satisfaction of
doing things cheaply, since they have sub-let
the dower-house to a prosperous stock-broker,
his wife being Mildred's cousin, who is content
to pay for the social advantages of the County,
and since George Ashton, who now has money
to spare, falls in with Mildred's view of justice
in the relation of owner and tenant. She is
radiant and triumphant and supremely happy.
Why should she not be? If you are a philosopher, remember that the qualities of sound sense,
directness of aim and action, and freedom from
all morbidity and sensibility, do mostly make
their possessors happy. And if you are a moral-

ist, remember that Mildred Ashton has many
virtues; she is a good wife and a good mother
and a popular hostess; if she is selfish it is an
enlarged selfishness which includes her husband
and children in its benevolence, if ever she
schemed unconsciously, it was for her home and
not for herself alone.

One may pity the sensitive and wayward without grudging Mrs. Jack her prosperity and
happiness. One may reflect that possibilities of
fineness in them are sometimes foiled, and such
fineness as they have is sometimes blurred or
turned aside by the rough accidents of the
world; one may regret that the rare chances
which come to them of rising to where the
coarser world cannot hinder them are most often
missed.

But these are not, it may be, the very elect,
between whom and Mildred Ashton they stand
halfway. Had they been finer and stronger,
perhaps the accidents of the world would not
have touched them. As it is, the world had
used them reasonably well, and so my narrative
ends happily.

A

List of Books

IN

BELLES LETTRES

JOHN LANE: THE BODLEY HEAD
140 FIFTH AVENUE
NEW YORK
1896

A

List of Books in Belles Lettres

ALLEN (GRANT).
THE LOWER SLOPES. With a Titlepage by J. ILLING-
WORTH KAY. Crown 8vo. $1.50.

> That Mr. Allen is a poet, quite individual, if limited, these ex-
> cursions leave no manner of doubt. — *Bookman* (*London*).
> The power of passionate and pointed utterance displayed in
> this little volume ought certainly not to be allowed to run to
> waste. — *Westminster Gazette* (*London*).

ATHERTON (GERTRUDE).
PATIENCE SPARHAWK AND HER TIMES. A Novel.
Crown 8vo. $1.50. [*In preparation.*

BEECHING (REV. H. C.).
ST. AUGUSTINE AT OSTIA: Oxford Sacred Poem.
Crown 8vo, wrappers. 50 cents.

> The work of a man of genuine poetic feeling and of erudition
> besides, who has known how to give a gracefully imaginative ren-
> dering to that struggle between conflicting ideas and faiths of
> which St. Augustine was the outcome. — *Times* (*London*).

BENNETT (E. A.).
A MAN FROM THE NORTH. A Novel. Crown 8vo.
$1.25. [*In preparation.*

BENSON (ARTHUR CHRISTOPHER).
LORD VYET AND OTHER POEMS. Fcap. 8vo. $1.25.

BROTHERTON (MARY).
ROSEMARY FOR REMEMBRANCE. With Titlepage and
Cover Design by WALTER WEST. Fcap. 8vo.
$1.25.

> A rarely beautiful little volume of verse. Suggests the work of
> one or two very famous women poets. — *Realm* (*London*).

BROWN (VINCENT).
TWO IN CAPTIVITY. A Novel. 16mo. 75 cents.
[*In preparation.*

CHAPMAN (ELIZABETH RACHEL).
    MARRIAGE QUESTIONS IN MODERN FICTION. Crown
       8vo. $1.50.   [*In preparation.*

CHARLES (JOSEPH F.).
    THE DUKE OF LINDEN. A Novel. Crown 8vo. $1.25.
                           [*In preparation.*

CRACKANTHORPE (HUBERT).
    VIGNETTES: a Miniature Journal of Whim and Sen-
       timent. Fcap. 8vo. Boards. $1.00.

CRANE (WALTER).
    TOY BOOKS. A Re-issue. Each with new Cover
       Designs and end papers. 25 cents each.
      I. Mother Hubbard.
      II. The Three Bears.
     III. The Absurd A B C.
    The group of three bound in one volume, with a deco-
       rative cloth cover, end papers, and a newly written
       and designed Titlepage and Preface. 4to. $1.25.

CROSKEY (JULIAN).
    MAX. A Novel. Crown 8vo. $1.50.
                       [*In preparation.*

CUSTANCE (OLIVE).
    LOVE'S FIRST FRUITS. Poems. Fcap. 8vo. $1.25.
                       [*In preparation.*

DAVIDSON (JOHN).
    NEW BALLADS. With a Titlepage and Cover Design
       by WALKER WEST. Fcap. 8vo. $1.50.

    BALLADS AND SONGS. With a Titlepage and Cover
       Design by WALTER WEST. Fcap. 8vo. $1.50.
                      [*Fourth edition.*

We must acknowledge that Mr. Davidson's work in this volume displays great power. . . . . There is strength and to spare. — *Times* (*London*).

Mr. Davidson's new book is the best he has done, and to say this, is a good deal. Here, at all events, is a poet who is never tame or dull; who, at all events, never leaves us indifferent. His verse speaks to the blood, and there are times when "the thing becomes a trumpet." — *Saturday Review* (*London*).

    A RANDOM ITINERARY AND A BALLAD. With a
       Frontispiece and Titlepage by LAURENCE HOUS-
       MAN. Fcap. 8vo. $1.50.

One part of "A Random Itinerary" should not be praised above the others. . . . . The whole volume is of wholesome flavour, and is beautiful withal. — *Literary World* (*London*).

DAVIDSON (JOHN), *continued*.

    PLAYS: An Unhistorical Pastoral ; A Romantic Farce ;
        Bruce, a Chronicle Play ; Smith, a Tragic Farce ;
        Scaramouch in Naxos, a Pantomime. With a Fron-
        tispiece and Cover Design by AUBREY BEARDSLEY.
        500 copies. Small 4to. $2.50.

      The best play in the present volume is entitled "Smith, a
Tragic Farce." The motive is as modern as Ibsen, the method is
as ancient as Shakespeare ; and yet, in spite of this incongruity,
the play must be pronounced a fine one. — *Liverpool Daily Post.*
      A notable volume. . . . . "The "Unhistorical Pastoral" is a
charming conception, delicately wrought. — *Saturday Review*
(*London*).

DAWSON (A. J.).

    MIDDLE GREYNESS. A Novel. Crown 8vo. $1.50.
                                  [*In preparation.*

EGERTON (GEORGE).

    SYMPHONIES. Crown 8vo. $1.00.   [*In preparation.*

EGLINTON (JOHN).

    TWO ESSAYS ON THE REMNANT. Post 8vo, wrappers.
        50 cents.   [*Second edition.*

      The appreciation of Wordsworth and the caustic criticism of
Goethe are particularly delightful, and from first to last the book
is simply a work of genius. — *Pall Mall Budget* (*London*).

FEA (ALLAN).

    THE FLIGHT OF THE KING. A full, true, and par-
        ticular Account of the Escape of His Most
        Sacred Majesty King Charles II., after the Battle
        of Worcester. With twelve Portraits in Photo-
        gravure, and nearly 100 other Illustrations. Demy
        8vo. $7. 50.

FIFTH (GEORGE).

    THE MARTYR'S BIBLE. A Novel. Crown 8vo. $1.50.
                                  [*In preparation.*

FLETCHER (J. S.).

    GOD'S FAILURES. Fcap. 8vo. $1.25.

    BALLADS OF REVOLT. Fcap. 8vo. $1.00.

FLOWERDEW (HERBERT).

    A CELIBATE'S WIFE. A Novel. Crown 8vo. $1.50.
                                  [*In preparation.*

GARNETT (RICHARD).

POEMS. With Titlepage by J. ILLINGWORTH KAY. Crown 8vo. $1.50.

A book of high poetic merit and charm. — *Academy (London)*.

DANTE, PETRARCH, CAMOENS, cxxiv Sonnets rendered in English. With Titlepage and Cover Design by PATTEN WILSON. Crown 8vo. $1.50.

Dr. Garnett once more shows his versatility and his gift of fine workmanship in verse by this book. — *Times (London)*.

Quite apart from their value as translations, Dr. Garnett's sonnets, Petrarchan in form but saturated with the Shakespearian spirit, form a notable contribution to the treasury of English poetic literature. — *Graphic (London)*.

GRIMSHAWE (BEATRICE).

BROKEN AWAY. A Novel. Crown 8o. $1.25.

[*In preparation.*

HAYES (ALFRED).

THE VALE OF ARDEN AND OTHER POEMS. With a Titlepage and Cover designed by E. H. NEW. Fcap. 8vo. $1.25.

Mr. Hayes is a refined writer of unpretentious verse, and his contented mood is sufficiently rare in modern poetry to make his volume notable. — *Daily Chronicle (London)*.

This little volume contains very beautiful workmanship. It is especially beautiful in the piece which gives its title to the volume. — *Daily News (London)*.

JAMES (W. P.).

ROMANTIC PROFESSIONS: A Volume of Essays. With Titlepage designed by J. ILLINGWORTH KAY. Crown 8vo. $1.50.

These essays are chiefly remarkable for the charm of their style and their wealth of illustration. The author's knowledge of fiction of all kinds, and his critical insight into the merits and demerits of writers of fiction, are considerable. — *Morning Post (London.)*

JOHNSTONE (C. E.).

BALLADS OF BOY AND BEAK. With a Titlepage by F. H. TOWNSEND. Square 32mo. 75 cents.

It is impossible to do other than covet the juvenile spirit of a grown-up poet who lingers so lovingly over the experiences of desk and playground, and whose every written page only lacks the inky smudge of the schoolboy-hand to make it perfect. — *Dundee Advertiser.*

LANDER (HARRY).

WEIGHED IN THE BALANCE. A Novel. Crown 8vo. $1.50.

LEFROY (EDWARD CRACROFT).

POEMS. With a Memoir by W. A. GILL, and a reprint of J. A. SYMOND's Critical Essay on ECHOES FROM THEOCRITUS. Crown 8vo. $1.50.

LE GALLIENNE (RICHARD).

THE QUEST OF THE GOLDEN GIRL. With a Cover designed by WILL H. BRADLEY. Crown 8vo. $1.50.

ENGLISH POEMS. Revised. Crown 8vo. Purple cloth. $1.50. [Fourth edition.

In "English Poems" rhyme, rhythm, and diction are worthy of a writer of ability and high ambition.—*Athenæum (London).*

There is plenty of accomplishment, there is abundance of tuneful notes, sentiment often very pleasing, delicacy, grace. . . . . The best thing in the book to one's own taste is the last half of "Sunset in the City." "Paolo and Francesca" is very clever. — Mr. ANDREW LANG, *in New Review (London).*

ROBERT LOUIS STEVENSON: An Elegy. And other Poems, mainly Personal. Crown 8vo. $1.50.

Few, indeed, could be more fit to sing the dirge of the "Virgil of prose" than the poet whose *curiosa felicitas* is so close akin to Stevenson's own charm. — *Daily Chronicle (London).*

LOCKE (W. J.).

DERELICTS. A Novel. Crown 8vo. $1.50.

LOWRY (H. D.).

MAKE BELIEVE. Illustrated by CHARLES ROBINSON. Crown 8vo. $1.50.

THE HAPPY EXILE. With etched Illustrations by E. PHILIP PIMLOTT. (Arcady Library.) Crown 8vo. $1.50.

MARZIALS (THEO.).

THE GALLERY OF PIGEONS AND OTHER POEMS. Post 8vo. $1.50.

Endless combinations of wonderfully vivid perceptions, and the picturesque inventions of a joyous fancy. Picturesque and vivid are only words — they are not definite enough to give a clear conception of the peculiar quality or the peculiar limits of the pleasure to be found in it. — *Academy (London).*

MEREDITH (GEORGE).

THE FIRST PUBLISHED PORTRAIT OF THIS AUTHOR. Engraved on the wood by W. BISCOMBE GARDNER, after the painting by G. F. WATTS. Proof copies on Japanese vellum, signed by Painter and Engraver. $7.50.

MEYNELL (ALICE).

THE CHILDREN. Fcap. 8vo. $1.25.

This is the first book printed at the Wayside Press, by Will H. Bradley.

POEMS. Fcap. 8vo. $1.25.   [*Third edition*.

To the metrical themes attempted by her she brings emotion, sincerity, together with an exquisite play upon our finer chords quite her own, not to be heard from another. Some of her lines have the living tremor in them. The poems are beautiful in idea as in grace of touch. — Mr. GEORGE MEREDITH, *in The National Review, August,* 1896.

She sings with a very human sincerity, a singular religious intensity — rare, illusive, curiously perfumed verse, so simple always, yet so subtle in its simplicity. — *Athenæum (London).*

THE RHYTHM OF LIFE AND OTHER ESSAYS. Fcap. 8vo. $1.25.   [*Third edition.*

Full of profound, searching, sensitive appreciation of all kinds of subjects. Exercises in close thinking and exact expression, almost unique in the literature of the day. —*Athenæum (London).*

I am about to direct attention to one of the very rarest products of nature and grace, — a woman of genius, one who I am bound to confess has falsified the assertion I made some time ago that no female writer of our time has attained to true "distinction." . . . . Mrs. Meynell has shown an amount of perceptive reason and ability to discern self-evident things as yet undiscerned, a reticence, fulness, and effectiveness of expression which place her in the very front rank of living writers in prose. At least half of the volume is classical work, embodying as it does new thought in perfect language, and bearing in every sentence the hall-mark of genius, namely, the marriage of masculine force of insight with feminine grace and tact of expression. — Mr. COVENTRY PATMORE, *in Fortnightly Review.*

THE COLOUR OF LIFE AND OTHER ESSAYS. Fcap. 8vo. $1.25.   [*Third edition.*

Mrs. Meynell's papers are little sermons, ideal sermons, — let no one uninstructed by them take fright at the title, — they are not preachments ; they are of the sermon's right length, about as long as the passage of a cathedral chant in the ear, and keeping thoughout to the plain step of daily speech, they leave a sense of stilled singing in the mind they fill. The writing is limpid in its depths. She must be a diligent reader of the Saintly Lives. Her manner presents to me the image of one accustomed to walk in holy places and keep the eye of a fresh mind on our tangled world, happier in observing than in speaking. And I can fancy Matthew Arnold lighting on such Essays as I have named, saying with refreshment, " She can write ! " It does not seem to me too bold to imagine Carlyle listening, without the weariful gesture, to his wife's reading of the same, hearing them to the end, and giving his comment, " That woman thinks." — Mr. GEORGE MEREDITH, *in The National Review, August,* 1896.

MAKOWER (STANLEY V.).

CECILIA. A Novel. Crown 8vo. $1.25.

OPPENHEIM (MICHAEL).

A HISTORY OF THE ADMINISTRATION OF THE ROYAL NAVY, and of Merchant Shipping in the relation to the Navy from MDIX. to MDCLX., with an Introduction treating of the earlier period. Plates. Demy 8vo. $7.50.

MILMAN (HELEN).

IN THE GARDEN OF PEACE. With Illustrations by EDMUND H. NEW. (Arcady Library.) Crown 8vo. $1.50. *[In preparation.*

ROBERTSON (JOHN M.).

ESSAYS TOWARDS A CRITICAL METHOD. (New Series.) Crown 8vo. $1.50. *[In preparation.*

ST. CYRES (LORD).

THE LITTLE FLOWERS OF ST. FRANCIS. A new rendering into English of the Fioretti di San Francesco. Crown 8vo. $1.50. *[In preparation.*

SEAMAN (OWEN).

THE BATTLE OF THE BAYS. With Titlepage and Cover Design by PATTEN WILSON. Fcap. 8vo. $1.25.

SETOUN (GABRIEL).

THE CHILD WORLD: Poems. Illustrated by CHARLES ROBINSON. Crown 8vo, gilt top. $1.50.

SHARP (EVELYN).

WYMPS: Fairy Tales. With 8 Coloured Illustrations and Decorative Cover by MABEL DEARMER. 4to. $1.75.

SHARP (LOUISA).

POEMS. With a Memoir by FREDERICK HARRISON. Fcap. 8vo. $1.50. *[In preparation.*

STEVENSON (ROBERT LOUIS).

PRINCE OTTO. A Rendering in French by EGERTON CASTLE. Crown 8vo. With Frontispiece, Titlepage, and Cover Design by D. Y. CAMERON. $2.50.

Also 50 copies on large paper, uniform in size with the Edinburgh Edition of the works. $7.50.

Mr. Egerton Castle's excellent translation of Stevenson's " Prince

STEVENSON (ROBERT LOUIS), *continued.*

Otto" will undoubtedly bring many new readers to the book. Is beautifully printed. — *Morning Post* (*London*).

To say that the French is worthy of the English is to pay it a compliment which is fully deserved. — *Yorkshire Herald.*

Mr. Castle's French is perfect, and he preserves in his translation all the virility of the author. — *Pall Mall Gazette* (*London*).

STREET (G. S.)

THE WISE AND THE WAYWARD. A Novel. Crown 8vo. $1.50.

TENNYSON (FREDERICK).

POEMS OF THE DAY AND YEAR. With a Titlepage designed by PATTEN WILSON. Crown 8vo. $1.50.

His soul is satisfied with the contemplation of beautiful things, and the utterance in flowing imagery of the emotions they excite in him. Lovers of pure poetry will find much to satisfy them. — *Daily Chronicle* (*London*).

He has no small share of the Tennysonian music, and in two points at least he falls short of no writer of his generation, — in his love of nature and in his belief in the dignity of the poet's function. — *Times* (*London*).

THIMM (CARL A.).

A COMPLETE BIBLIOGRAPHY OF FENCING AND DUEL-LING, as Practiced by all European Nations from the Middle Ages to the Present Day. With a Classified Index, arranged Chronologically accord-ing to Languages. Illustrated with numerous Portraits of Ancient and Modern Masters of the Art. Titlepages and Frontispieces of some of the earliest works. Portrait of the Author by WILSON STEER, and Titlepage designed by PATTEN WILSON. 4to. $7.50.

THOMPSON (FRANCIS).

POEMS. With Frontispiece, Titlepage, and Cover Design by LAURENCE HOUSMAN. Post 4to. $1.50.   [*Fourth edition.*

I can hardly doubt that at least that minority who can recognise the essentials under the accidents of poetry, and who feel that it is to poetic Form only, and not to forms, that eternity belongs, will agree that, alike in wealth and dignity of imagination, in depth and subtlety of thought, and in magic and mastery of language, a new poet of the first rank is to be welcomed in the author of this volume. — Mr. H. D. TRAILL, *in Nineteenth Century.*

Profound thought and far-fetched splendour of imagery, and nimble-witted discernment of those analogies which are the roots of the poet's language, abound. . . . . Qualities which ought to place him, even should he do no more than he has done, in the prominent ranks of fame, with Cowley and Crawshaw. — Mr. COVENTRY PATMORE, *in Fortnightly Review.*

THOMPSON (FRANCIS), *continued*.

SISTER SONGS. An Offering to Two Sisters. With Frontispiece, Titlepage, and Cover Design by LAURENCE HOUSMAN. Post 4to. Buckram. $1.50.

Mr. Thompson is the only one of the young poets of the day who peristently tempts one, page after page, to waive one's critic right, and contentedly to stand and admire. — *Academy (London)*.

If any were uncertain, after the publication of Mr. Thompson's "Poems," that a new star was added to the galaxy, the splendid succession of which has never failed in the English poetic firmament, let them read "Sister Songs" and be assured. — *Speaker (London)*.

TRAILL (H. D.).

THE BARBAROUS BRITISHERS. A Tip-top Novel. With Title and Cover Design by AUBREY BEARDSLEY. Crown 8vo, wrapper. 50 cents.

Nothing funnier has been written.— *Daily Telegraph (London)*.

A cleverer or more genuinely mirth-provoking, and withal useful parody, we have not read for many a long day. A very large circulation may be predicted. — *St. James's Gazette (London)*.

TYNAN (KATHARINE HINKSON).

CUCKOO SONGS. With Titlepage by LAURENCE HOUSMAN. Fcap. 8vo. $1.25.

Enchantingly simple, innocent, and light, a book of aerial music in delicate cadencies. — *Illustrated London News*.

WALTON AND COTTON.

THE COMPLEAT ANGLER, a new Edition of. Edited by RICHARD LE GALLIENNE. Illustrated by EDMUND H. NEW. 4to. $6.00.

It would have been difficult to have selected an artist to illustrate this work more in sympathy with it than Mr. New is proving himself to be. This edition shows every promise of being one of the most desirable to possess of this quaint and admirable work.— *Studio (London)*.

Copiously illustrated and exquisitely printed, it promises to be "a thing of beauty and a joy for ever" to book lovers who value alike intrinsic excellence and a fair exterior. — *Publishers' Circular (London)*.

WATSON (H. B. MARRIOTT).

THE CAREER OF DELIA HASTINGS. Crown 8vo. $1.50.   [*In preparation*.

WATT (FRANCIS).

THE LAWS LUMBER ROOM. Second series. Fcap. 8vo. $1.25.   [*In preparation*.

WHYTE (WALTER).
    LESLIE WARDEN. A Novel. Crown 8vo. $1.50.
                                  [*In preparation.*

THE YELLOW BOOK.
    AN ILLUSTRATED QUARTERLY. Small 4to. $1.50
      each volume.
        Vol. I., of which Four Editions were issued, is
          now out of print.
        Vol. II. Third Edition.   [*A few copies remain.*

The second volume is better than the first. — *Daily Chronicle* (*London*).
   A decided improvement on the first. — *Daily Telegraph* (*London*).

        Vol. III. Third Edition.

A considerable improvement on its predecessors. — *Speaker* (*London*).

        Vol. IV. Second Edition.

On the whole, the new "Yellow Book" has more that is attractive and less that is repellant than any of its predecessors. — *Globe* (*London*).

        Vol. V. Second Edition.

This "Yellow Book" has left its predecessors far behind in general interest. — *Daily Chronicle* (*London*).

        Vol. VI. Second Edition.

None of the other five volumes have reached the mark of excellence attained by the sixth. From all points of view the "Yellow Book" seems to improve quarterly. — *Vanity Fair* (*London*).

        Vol. VII. Second Edition.

The new "Yellow Book" need not fear the rivalry of any of its predecessors. — *Daily Chronicle* (*London*).

        Vol. VIII. Second Edition.

The eighth number is far the best that has yet appeared. — *St. James's Gazette* (*London*).

        Vol. IX. Second Edition.

This number of the "Yellow Book" is likely to be one of the most popular. — *Globe* (*London*).

        Vol. X. Second Edition.

A particularly strong number. — *Gentlewoman* (*London*).

        Vol. XI. Small 4to. $1.50.   [*Just ready.*

Mr. Lane is the sole agent for the sale in America of the books issued from the Vale Press, all of which are printed under the supervision of the well-known English artist CHARLES RICKETTS. *The following books are now ready :*

THE POEMS OF SIR JOHN SUCKLING.
Edited by JOHN GRAY. With Honeysuckle Border and Initial Letters designed and cut on the wood by CHARLES RICKETTS. Demy 8vo. $7.50 *net.*

EPICURUS, LEONTION, AND TERNISSA.
By WALTER SAVAGE LANDOR. With a Border designed and cut on the wood by CHARLES RICKETTS. Crown 8vo. $3.50 *net.*

THE EARLY POEMS OF JOHN MILTON.
Reprinted from the edition seen through the press by the author. With a Frontispiece, Border, and Initial Letters designed and cut on the wood by CHARLES RICKETTS. Crown 4to. $10.00 *net.*

SPIRITUAL POEMS.
By JOHN GRAY. With a Frontispiece, Border, and Cover designed and cut on the wood by CHARLES RICKETTS. Crown octavo. $4.00 *net.*

These books are among the most beautiful produced this century. Only a very few copies are printed for America. Prospectuses on application.

www.ingramcontent.com/pod-product-compliance
Lightning Source LLC
Chambersburg PA
CBHW022006050726
47499CB00006BB/1720